Songs of the Deliverer

A Modern Day Story of Christ

By Elvo Fortunato Bucci

ISBN: 978-1499134544

Original Songs by Elvo, Mark, and Domenic Bucci

Cover Art by Susan Berry

Editor: Blair H. Bucci

First Edition published: 7-14

PRELUDE

Evil greeted salvation in the manger.

The thunder of galloping horses shook the earth as the soldiers rampaged into town. Trembling in their shelters, the peasants pleaded among themselves for the soldiers to ride on. They had heard talk of the King's commandment. They knew how he feared the prophecy. Having borne the pain of his brutal cruelty throughout his reign, they considered escape for they were helpless against his vast army. Yet, they stayed for they believed that not even this King was capable of such horror. Ride on, they prayed.

And still the thunder roared.

The prophecy—oh, how it tormented him. He was their King, as was his father before him, and yet these pitiful fools laid in wait for a new born king that had been ascribed by Scripture. For years, he saw how they gathered in worship for this new savior to rescue them. They searched skyward for help, ignorant that on this land he was their lord and master. He fed them, he kept them secure, he provided for them. For all he had done, all he had gained was scorn.

Then he was visited by the magic men. Three supposed wise men who looked to the stars for their premonitions.

Here they were in his palace bejeweled in their flamboyant garments and speaking of some guiding star that was leading them to the anointed one. They were sure that the star would take them to the new born messiah. Pompous in their knowledge, the King quickly saw they could be tools to end his search for his presumed successor. He drew them in.

Magnificent news, he inveighed. He bathed them in praise for their prescience. He promised to provide for their every need for this grandest of journeys. He would even have two of his most accomplished guards escort them to ensure their safe travel. To the last, they cautiously objected but the King appealed to their arrogance by citing the vast import of their calling. They acceded to his wish.

Secretly, the King told the guards what their real task was to be.

The magic men rode off with their appointed escorts in pursuit of the star. Many days later, a single guard dismally returned.

The guard told the King that they had traveled to the outskirts of a little town called Bethlehem. The magic men said they would spend the night in the field before entering town at daybreak. As they prepared for sleep, the magic men offered the guards wine from their flasks which they pronounced to be of very special vintage. After consuming the wine, the guard could only recall blearily waking late the next day when the sun was high in the sky. The magic men had vanished and left no trail. Terrified of reprisal for failing the King, the other guard fled the country. The returning guard confessed their failure and offered his life in repentance. With one furious thrust of his sword, the incensed King took it.

The King seethed at the utter incompetence of his mercenaries. He raged at the notion that the three jesters had duped him and had denied him his conquest. Frothing on the throne came a plan only hate could conceive.

So simple, he reasoned, and yet so certain.

The King called upon his General and told him of the mission. The General stood stupefied at the words he was hearing. So that there would be no confusion, the King repeated the directive and declared that there would be no exception and he could leave no doubt. The General snapped to attention, hailed his commander, and briskly marched off to gather his men. Within hours, a legion of brass-armored centurions bore down upon their unwitting targets.

Late into the night with only a single star lighting the blackened sky, the soldiers rode. Charging into town, the marauders came to a rickety inn. Startling the innkeeper from his sleep, the General demanded to be taken to the occupants. The petrified man took them room by room to each of the building's inhabitants: a slothful drunkard disoriented from his indulgence, a heavily bearded elder atop his hired woman, two brothers who had been working in town for months preparing for bed, and the innkeeper's wife and her frail mother sitting quietly in a barren room reading Scripture. The General eyed the man skeptically. He impatiently asked about children.

The innkeeper stammered that there were no children. The General paused in confusion and then turned to mount his horse. He huddled with his lieutenants to devise the tactics by which they would inflict their wrath. Frightened for what the King's army intended for the children, the innkeeper told the two brothers he was housing to rush into town. They slipped out the back and began to frantically spread the news of the impending assault.

Forewarned, the families nevertheless remained soundlessly in their homes, as if their silence would hide them in plain sight. No evil could be so profound as to take their babies. Not even this vile King whose only truth was hatred; whose singular ambition was to doom the prophecy so that his kingdom alone would endure, not even he would be so malevolent as to terrorize helpless children.

For years, the King had agonized over the prophecy of the newborn prince: 'the Lord will send a sign, a young woman is with child and shall bear a son and shall name him Emmanuel—God is with us.' What insolent god would dare attempt to seize the throne from his grasp, he would rail endlessly. Now, at last, the demise of the prophecy approached in unison with the stampede of his ruthless army legion.

And on the thunder roared.

Into town they rode finally stopping at a row of humble dwellings shuttered for the night. Chastened by his failure at the inn, the General was determined to fulfill his commands lest he, too, became a fatal target of the King's ire.

Dismounting, he barged into the first home finding a family huddled together as if they knew of the assault he was leading. So be it, he thought, my purpose is more easily served if they are all quaking in fear.

He surveyed the room seeing a man he assumed to be the father, his wife, a young boy nearly as tall as the father, and a little girl. The King had told him the child of the prophecy was likely to be very young or even new born. The General, not being a father, did not know how to recognize a child's age. An aide told him that if the child spoke in sentences that meant they were too old for their wicked purposes.

He pushed past the boy and walked to the girl. He prodded her by poking his fingers into her chest. Her father jumped up to protect his daughter only to be clubbed by one of the centurions. Collapsing unconscious to the floor, the mother screamed in panic. The girl rushed to her father's side. She took her father's head and laid it in her lap. She began to sing the lullaby they sung before bed in an attempt to sooth his injury. The General shook his head upon hearing her clear articulation. Too old, he determined.

Reluctantly, he turned to leave. The mother, thinking his departure was a measure of mercy, bowed and gave praise to the invaders.

Then the General heard a noise, a chirp really. He stopped abruptly. He scanned the dwelling and heard the noise once more. He saw the mother contort her body in an attempt to shield a basket in the corner of the room. Menacingly, he approached the basket. He bent down to remove the white cloth covering it. The mother grabbed his hand; two soldiers wrenched her away and firmly held her down on the ground. The General pulled away the covering. Inside the basket was a baby; a boy, he thought.

Was this the one? Could this wisp of life be the mighty savior the prophecy had foretold? Was this the future ruler whose coming had long tormented his King?

The mother pleaded desperately with the General not to take the baby from her. He looked at her oddly. His commandment from the King was not to take, it was to kill. Every child in the town living under the guiding star the magic men had followed, every child who could be the fulfillment of the prophecy, every child of this forlorn place that could be the coming messiah, every child whose birth threatened the dominion of the King; all these children were to die and with their deaths all hazards to the King's throne vanquished.

He drew his blade from its sheath, brandished it in front of the panicked mother, and plunged it through the heart of the infant.

Shrieks of anguish engulfed the home. He withdrew the sword from the tiny corpse and signaled to his men to ride on. And on the murdering soldiers rode. From home to home, family to family, hate raged as the blood of babes flowed through the town. For every child judged a threat, a death was paid in the massacre of innocents.

Finally, the atrocities came to an end. Exhausted from their purge with their horses gasping for air, the centurions departed.

As they were exiting town, the General again saw the innkeeper. Leave no doubt, the King had commanded. He leaned down from his horse and grabbed the innkeeper by the throat: children?

Choking and barely able to make a sound, the dispirited man looked onto the General's blood-spattered face and just shook his head from side to side. The General released his grip and turned away. He was about to leave when, from the corner of his eye, he noticed a flame from behind the inn. He turned his gaze towards the source of the light. The innkeeper nervously realized he had seen the manger.

He uneasily explained that a young couple had earlier ridden in on their mule and were staying in the manger as he had no place for them at the inn.

Again the General bellowed: children?

The innkeeper fell to his knees, sobbing. He begged for mercy but the General had been instructed that there would be no mercy and there could be no doubt. He motioned to his soldiers.

There in the manger, the three magic men knelt before the mother to greet her new born babe with gifts of gold, frankincense, and myrrh. In her arms, she held the baby—the one to whom they had been guided by the star's light. Her husband took a dampened cloth and cooled her face. It had been a difficult pregnancy. Their travel to this place was long and the journey harsh. Yet here, at last, she lay with her baby caressing his dark brown hair, lovingly kissing his cheek, just as she had dreamed. In her dream she was told that she would bear a child who is the Son of God and he would bring great joy to her and to all the people. A child sent to save the world who would be called Jesus, savior and deliverer. Holding him now, all she knew was that this was her baby and she was his mother.

And then through the flame burning, she saw the face of evil enter the manger. Instinctively, she pulled the baby tightly to her chest. Her husband stood as he saw the unwelcomed intruders come nearer. The magic men turned and saw the General and his minions, recognizing their allegiance to the King. Silently, the General came to the mother. He looked down upon her as she lay in the bed of straw. He noted the youthfulness of the mother and witnessed the new born boy she held in her arms. He remembered the prophecy: 'a young woman is with child and shall bear a son.'

Knowingly, he gestured to his soldiers. Two of them rushed to seize the startled husband and threw him violently to the ground, immobilizing him while he struggled vainly to escape. Five more encircled the magic men, though there was no risk of aggression from these feeble purveyors of mysticism. He bent down and looked curiously at the child. He nodded and patted the baby gently on the head. Then he put both hands around the baby and pulled him away from the mother's grasp. She reached for the captor and scratched his arm in a futile effort to keep her baby. The General held the baby outright with his massive hands fully encompassing the boy's tiny body. Weak and terrified, she tried to rise but fell once more in her hopeless struggle to save her son.

The General stepped towards the crossing wooden beams that secured the roof of the manger. With one arm, he braced the baby on the cross. With the other, he drew his blade, still dripping with the blood of the slaughtered innocents. The persecutor stared blankly into the face of salvation. The baby's eyes tilted skyward as if to ask a question.

Is this the day?

The General raised his weapon. The mother cried out in agony: my God, my God, why have you forsaken me? He methodically lowered the blade and laid the steel tip on the baby's breast. He cautiously and callously pierced the soft skin surrounding the ribcage causing a single drop of blood to spill. He paused to consider his task, ignorant to the wild shrieks and wailing about him. Soullessly, he pushed the blade into the baby's chest perforating his lung.

The boy exhaled a final time. Then with one last, horrid and hateful thrust, he impaled the infant with his sword leaving the baby to hang in oblivion on the cross post.

There they were together in this time: a king and his henchmen, a persecuted people, three wise men, a mother and her newborn son—the Savior of the world—crucified on the cross.

CHAPTER ONE

It began with a word, and the word called for deliverance, and the word was deliverance.

He stepped into the darkness which inhabited the world. He was in the world though the world was not in him. He had come to bring light. He was the light.

He was sent on a sacred mission to seek the lost, heal the broken, awaken the hopeless, and free the enslaved. And to all, he would reveal the one true way home. For this sovereign purpose, he pledged his life. Here, in this day, it was time.

He began to walk.

His walk eventually took him to the end of a gloomy, narrow road. He heard noises. He looked and saw a bright neon sign spelling out the name of a local tavern. In the parking lot, a man lay cowering under the branches of a leafless tree. A big, brawny attacker staggered towards the fallen one, picked him up, and threw him against the tree trunk. The oppressor hollered in slurred, unintelligible speech. He lifted the vagrant and tossed him into a parked car. Still not satisfied with his abuse, he grabbed the victim's collar with one hand while he cocked the fist of the other hand and readied to pummel the face of his defenseless target.

Trapped and hopeless, the beggar called out the word that would gain his deliverance, "Help," he said and then, "God, help me."

The fist was stopped before it hit the beggar's face. The drunken mugger tossed the beggar aside and turned around in bewilderment. He shook loose his thick arm from the street walker and pushed the stranger in the chest. The walker didn't respond. The intoxicated offender took a moment to survey this interloper standing before him in the light; a smaller man wearing faded gray jeans and a white cotton pullover sweatshirt with the hood drawn over his head. Dismissively, he renewed his attack and rushed forward. Once more, he was stopped by the outstretched arm of the mystery man.

Confused and breathless, he looked at his adversary. He decided to make another assault. He lowered his shoulders and barreled ahead crying out loudly as he charged. Again, he somehow missed his prey and he fell hard into the side of the tavern's brick wall. Dazed and beaten, he rolled onto his back, tried vainly to get up, then collapsed and lay still in the night.

The beggar looked up into the light. The one who came for him took the beggar's hand and raised him up. He pulled out a cloth from the front center pocket of his pullover and wiped the blood from the beggar's face. He guided the lost man away from his torment and together they walked. After a while, they climbed the concrete steps of the place from where he had begun his walk, opened the door to go inside, and left the world behind.

They entered a large, open room with rows of single beds filling the space. An empty bed was located and the guest was guided to it. As he laid his head upon the thin pillow, the man looked to his savior and asked, "Who are you?"

The walker pulled the hood off his head uncovering his narrow face, days-old beard, and close-cropped hair. "Who do you say I am?" he asked in response. The beggar shrugged his shoulders, shut his eyes, and fell quickly to sleep.

After the new guest was made safe in his stead, the walker went up two flights of stairs. He entered the third floor and strode through the hallway. Hearing footsteps coming down the hall, the on-duty nurse jumped out of her chair and marched towards the noise. She immediately recognized the man and nodded her assent.

Down the hall, he walked. Quietly, he opened the door to a patient's room. He came to the bedside. The old women lying in the bed was staring vacantly at the soundless television. He touched her gently on the shoulder. She turned her head and saw his face. She smiled and cupped her hand on his cheek.

"My son."

He took her hand and sat with her. Her words were few and her thoughts were muddled. She was not the mother of his youth but she was the mother he would always love. Here she would spend her final days and he would remain with her as she remained with him.

He had brought her here when it was clear that she could no longer care for herself. Together, they came to this place. He told her they were moving into a new home, very large, with people to cook for them, and with many friends around. This place, their home, was a shelter for the homeless and the unwanted. The lower floor was for the men, the second floor was for the women and the third floor was for the manic and the demented. There were medical personnel, including nurses and a visiting physician, who would provide custodial and palliative care.

The television was on because she didn't like to be alone, though there was little she understood of it. At the sight of her son, she became alert and cheery. She took his hand and her eyes widened. As if for the first time, she asked him with excitement: "Have I told you about the dream?"

He nodded yes. Sadly, she turned away. A minute later, she turned to him and repeated, "Have I told you about the dream?"

Her son told her she should sleep but she turned away in disappointment. Just then, a news item came on the television. The broadcaster talked about a new musician touring the area who was gaining a devoted following across the State. He was called Jona.

The broadcaster said Jona would be performing tomorrow at the band shell at the park along the river. Thousands of young people drawn to Jona by his songs were expected to attend the concert. The report also noted the concern of government officials who believed this new voice could provoke rebellion against the authorities.

A picture of Jona was shown and it caught her attention. She looked at it closely and said, "Jona…yes, I remember him. I visited his mother once. Oh…" Her son looked curiously at her as she turned and shuffled through her old purse that lay on the table next to her bed. Finally, she found something and handed it to her son.

"See…this is when I visited her." It was a small black and white photograph of his mother and another young woman, Jona's mother, arm in arm, smiling joyfully.

He looked at it for some time. She put her hand over his and said, "Go see him."

He nodded and placed the photo in his pocket.

The television announcer concluded the segment by saying that many of Jona's fans believed he was the answer to their pleas for mercy and compassion in their lives. Some, he added, had even gone so far as to call Jona, 'the one.'

She spoke adamantly at the television saying, "No, you're wrong. He's not the one."

Then the woman turned to face her son.

"Emmanuel," she proclaimed, "you are."

CHAPTER TWO

The next day, the man whom Emmanuel saved woke up from his sleep. He lifted himself up, looked warily at his new surroundings, and saw his guardian.

Again, he asked: "Who are you?"

"I'm the one who came for you."

"You came for me?"

"You're Nathan, who I found under the tree."

The confused man nodded his head and asked, "What you did for me last night; how did you…"

"You will see greater things than that," Emmanuel interjected.

"When?"

"Follow me."

A mile from the shelter was a spacious park set across a great river. On most days, during the months that the weather permitted, people would gather for play or for leisure. On this day, the park was filled with anticipation for a special event. This was the annual "Festival of Spring" to celebrate the beginning of the season. A concert was about to be held at the band shell that faced the river. Thousands of people had entered the park to find a place on the lawn in front of the stage. They were a younger crowd, mostly teenagers and young adults, but there were some older adults and a few senior citizens. They were excited to hear this newcomer to the music scene.

Backstage, he prepared by tuning his guitar and then checking the amplifiers. He rehearsed in his mind the songs he would play. He could make adjustments to the show anytime he chose since he would be alone on the stage.

Periodically, he would gaze out to the gathering crowd. The crowds were getting bigger with each performance. It had only been a short time since he started doing the concerts. At first, few came to listen, sometimes no one at all. He hadn't really thought about the type of crowds he would attract, and it wasn't about making money. One moment, it just came to him. And at that moment, Jona left behind the life he had and began to sing.

As the crowds grew, so did the attention from the media. Reporters started to attend his concerts and give news accounts of the show. As the interest from the media grew, so did the interest from the authorities. His songs emboldened his supporters and they took his message back to their homes and communities. They followed him and they believed in him and in his message. But the government was suspicious of him.

He surveyed the crowd again. Out above the river, he saw clouds forming as the wind swirled briskly. People were getting impatient with their waiting and were shouting:

"Jona, Jona, Jona!"

Finally, he nodded to his two helpers. The stage lights came on.

The crowd erupted in applause. He came on stage wearing a leather vest and a floppy, wide-brimmed hat. Alone, he sat on a wooden stool and looked out into the eager crowd. He took his guitar and positioned it in his arms. The fans hushed. He began to strum the guitar and his song rang out:

Roar thunder for my freedom,
Rain lightning through my soul.
Give me courage and the faith
To battle on.

From the wilderness I'll shout,
Hear my message singing out:
Love, love, love
Wins the war.

See the light reveal the way,
All hail the newborn babe.
He's the path to righteousness
Salvation nears.

Repent of all your sin,
Are you ready to begin?
Hear Gabriel's horn
New life is born.

Congregate and consecrate,
Time to sanctify.
Baptize tonight
Let sin die.
God gives his Son to you
To deliver life anew.
Hey, listen everyone,
The Deliverer comes.

See the Word made to flesh.
Hear the truth and just say, yes.
Heaven shines on those who pray,
Our Savior reigns.

We are called to live life free,
Free to call God our King.
His Kingdom come, his will be done,

The Deliverer comes.

Congregate and consecrate,
Time to sanctify.
Baptize tonight
Let sin die.
God gives his Son to you
To deliver life anew.
Hey, listen everyone,
The Deliverer comes.

Roar thunder for my freedom,
Rain lightning through my soul.
Give me courage and the faith
To battle on.

We are called to live life free,
Free to call God our King.
His Kingdom come, the war is won,
The Deliverer comes.

Singing love, love, love
The Deliverer comes!

Singing love!

Bringing love!

He is love, love, love
The Deliverer comes!

He finished the song and his fans rose in raucous applause. He played on into the night, song after song, singing a message of hope and salvation. The clouds that had formed over the water earlier had now moved onto the shore and rain fell across the park. He bridged from the penultimate song into a repeat of the opening to close the show with another rendition of "The Deliverer Comes."

The rain began pouring down harder from the clouds and the crowd hurriedly scattered to escape the heavy rainfall and booming thunder. A streak of lightning flashed across the evening sky. The stage lights flickered and then exploded in radiant sparks. For a moment, he was blinded. And then emerging from the light, a man came on stage.

"I've been sent to you."

Jona, wincing from the blazing light, looked into the man's eyes. Stammering, he began to reply, "Are you, I mean, you are…"

"My mother was a friend of your mother." The man reached into his pocket and gave Jona the picture.

Jona looked at the face of his mother embracing a woman he did not recognize. Then he remembered. "My mother had told me about a young woman she met when she was pregnant with me. This woman was pregnant herself. She told me that the young woman had told her about a dream and in her dream she would bear a son. And this son would be…" Jona looked at the picture again and then at the man and said, "Are you…"

"I am Emmanuel."

"Emmanuel. The name that means, 'God is with us,'" Jona said. He continued to grip the picture. "I was so young when my mother told me that story. That was so long ago. Where have you been?"

"My time is coming," Emmanuel replied. He looked at Jona and said, "The songs you sing, the message you send, your testimony is true and your witness is powerful." He placed his hand upon Jona's shoulder, "You cleanse and purify with your songs. Do the same for me."

Jona shook his head. "No. I'm just a singer. I'm not anyone special."

Emmanuel bowed his head and said, "Jona, baptize me."

Jona repeated, "I'm not worthy to anoint you." Silently,

Emmanuel fell to his knees with his head still bowed.

Jona took a deep breath and lifted his eyes. He placed his hand on Emmanuel's forehead as the rain washed over them. He cried out into the raging storm: "Behold, Emmanuel! Those born of the world know worldly things but the one sent from above is above all. Bless he who is cleansed of sin and pure of heart. God is with us!"

Together, they held the stage. Then suddenly, they heard the sounds of sirens blaring from outside the park. Jona turned his head towards the jarring noise. The sounds were rapidly coming closer. The people in the crowd who were still left heard the noise, too, and scurried away from the park so as not to be caught up in the forthcoming police raid. They knew the stories of past concerts where the police had charged through the crowd indiscriminately battering some and arresting others. Jona gave a wry glance to Emmanuel knowing what was about to come. Emmanuel looked toward the approaching persecutors. His eyes tilted skyward as if to ask a question:

Is this the day?

Then Emmanuel looked back at Jona and said, "Follow me."

Jona said, "No, I'm not running from them anymore. They chase me like a swarm of snakes whenever I sing and it's time for me to take a stand. They feel threatened by me. They say I'm inciting civil disobedience but I have no interest in that. They say I'm undermining the government and its authority. I have no intention to undermine their authority. I am only telling the people to reclaim their own authority to seek and serve God."

He gestured for his helpers to come forward. A man came out from the shadows with a boy close behind him. Jona introduced them to Emmanuel.

"This is Jamie and this is his brother, Jonny. They've been traveling with me, helping me with the show. They're my friends. Take them with you."

Emmanuel nodded. Jona embraced Jamie and reached

down and hugged the boy. "This is Emmanuel. Do what he says."

Jona looked over the stage and out into where the crowds had been. "They said I was a superstar, someone who would lead the people. But I knew that wasn't me. My role is to prepare the way for one who follows. 'Make way for the one who existed before time, the one who is greater than all.' Those are the words that came to me. Now, that's the message I sing: cleanse your soul of sin and be baptized in the truth." He examined Emmanuel. "You're the one, aren't you?"

They heard the sirens now entering the park. Nathan took Emmanuel by the arm and pulled him off-stage.

After the four of them got far from the band shell, they turned and looked back. Multiple police cars had encircled the stage and several policemen grabbed Jona, assaulted him repeatedly, and threw him viciously into the back of a paddy wagon and sped off.

The stage was vacant except for Jona's headless hat flailing about in the wind.

The next morning, Jamie and Jonny awoke in their new surroundings. As they surveyed the place, Emmanuel came over with Nathan at his side. He told them Nathan would introduce them to the others. Then he looked at the young boy.

"Do you go to school?"

The boy shook his head, no.

"How will you learn?"

Faintly, Jonny replied: "I read. And I write."

Emmanuel glanced at his older brother who nodded in agreement.

"What do you write?"

"I write about what I see and what I hear. And I write about the things that happen. In here." Jonny reached into his jacket pocket and pulled out a well-worn journal and displayed pages and pages of his writing to Emmanuel.

Emmanuel assessed the journal then asked, "Why?"

Jonny replied, "So people will know the truth."

Emmanuel reflected for a moment and said, "Yes. You will follow me and write what happens."

Then he pronounced:

"You will be a witness to the truth."

CHAPTER THREE

They walked to the entrance of the Temple and Emmanuel was told to speak with Rabbi Nicholas about registering Jonny for weekly religious lessons. After questioning the boy for several minutes in private, the Rabbi skeptically approached Emmanuel.

"He tells me about his travels with a famous singer, a man named Jona, who purifies people of their sins. He says the singer, this Jona, is a messenger sent to prepare the way for someone greater to follow who will tell of new life to be born. I'm very curious, how does a child this young come up with such a bizarre story?"

"Perhaps because it is so," Emmanuel replied.

The Rabbi paused then said, "You come to this Temple to have the boy taught about Moses and the law and yet he is filled with ideas that blaspheme the sacred teachings. Who does that serve?"

"Who does one serve but God?" replied Emmanuel.

"Indeed," said the Rabbi, "but you do not serve God when you instill preposterous stories into the minds of children that rebuke the Scriptures."

Emmanuel answered, "Scripture warns of those 'who hear but do not understand, who see but do not perceive,' but you, a man dedicated to the law and the prophets, fail to heed its counsel. Who is rebuking Scripture now?"

The Rabbi stared intently at Emmanuel and said, "I can tell you are a learned man, yet you tell of things not known by man. Tell me, how can one be born again to new life?"

"You are a learned man who testifies to Moses seeing God in the burning bush," Emmanuel said, "but tell me if you will preach of my testimony.

"God loves the world and gives his Son so that those who believe in him will not die but shall be born to life everlasting."

The Rabbi responded, his voice now trembling, "I have spent my life in worship of God and in devotion to the law knowing what I know and saying what I say. Your teaching is difficult. Is it that you speak in parables?"

"I speak in truth. It is your will to see the light or be condemned to the darkness."

"And what of God's will? Does he cast off into the abyss those who fail to see this saving light that you talk about? Is that the aim of a righteous God: to forsake those who succumb to the temptation of evil?"

"Evil is not a seduction; it's a choice. It is not God's will to condemn. It is those who fail to follow the light who condemn themselves."

"You speak of this light as if it shines so freely upon us all. You make it sound like we are all just arms-length from the sun."

Emmanuel reached out his arm and placed it on Nicholas' shoulder. "Rabbi, the light from God's Son does shine freely upon all. Hear, see, and believe."

Emmanuel turned his back and walked away from the Temple.

Nicholas stood in stunned silence before shouting,

"Who are you?"

CHAPTER FOUR

Emmanuel was sitting with his mother as she lay peacefully in her bed when Jonny quietly walked into the room. After a while, the boy finally spoke:

"I was going to a wedding this week, but now it's not going to happen."

"Then you will stay here," replied Emmanuel.

The boy shook his head vigorously and cried, "You don't understand!"

Emmanuel's mother woke up at the sound of their conversation and looked at the boy in the room with her son. She asked softly, "Who is this boy?"

"This is Jonny. He lives with us in our home."

She said, "Uh-huh. What does he want?"

"He was about to tell us that," Emmanuel said as he turned to speak to Jonny. "What don't I understand?"

Jonny wiped his eyes and told them the reason for his sadness.

"My friend from religion class has a brother who is getting married this week. She said I could go to the wedding with them but then today they said she is really sick and had to go to the hospital. They said it was an emergency."

The boy laid his head on the shoulder of Emmanuel's mother and wept in her embrace.

The mother placed her hand affectionately on the boy's curly black hair.

"No need to be so sad," she said. "Everything will be fine." She put her hand on the boy's chin and raised it so he could see her. "My son will help."

The boy spun his head around and said to Emmanuel, "You will?"

Emmanuel clenched his teeth but did not answer. His mother looked at the boy and said, "Do what he says."

"I will. I'll take you to where my friend is," and he took Emmanuel's hand and began to walk out of the room.

Emmanuel resisted, saying to the woman, "Mother, this isn't the time."

"My son," she said, "this is for what you were born."

Emmanuel stood and regarded the woman who gave her life to him. He leaned over the bed and kissed her on the cheek.

Emmanuel and Jonny left her room. As they exited, they passed by an adjoining room. They could see an old man in the bed looking haggard and in noticeable pain. The name on the door said, "Simon." The old man saw Emmanuel, but turned away from him.

The hospital was nearby and as they got to the room where Jonny's friend was, they saw a woman in the hallway. The woman saw Jonny and reached down to hug him.

She lifted her eyes and said, "I'm Matilda. I'm a volunteer religion teacher at the Temple. Jonny is one of my students. He has been doing very well in the few weeks he has been with us."

"He tells me his friend is very sick."

Matilda cupped her hand over her mouth and nodded. "Jasmine is such a sweet and wonderful girl. She was diagnosed with an illness called sickle cell anemia a year ago. She has been struggling with it and this week it got worse. She is in a lot of pain and is not doing well. I can't imagine the anguish her family is going through. This was supposed to be a happy time for them with her brother's wedding, but now…" She turned away in tears.

When they entered the hospital room, they saw Jasmine's grandmother keeping vigil over her granddaughter. She saw them enter the room and said, "I'm sorry but Jasmine needs rest now. You have to go."

Jasmine lifted her head slightly to see who had entered the room. "No, Grandma. It's alright. This is my friend, Jonny. Let him stay. Please," she said feebly. The old woman nodded.

Jonny impulsively told the girl, "Jasmine, this is Emmanuel. He came here with me to help you."

The grandmother looked dubiously at Emmanuel. Jonny continued talking, "Do what he says and he'll make you better."

The grandmother interrupted and spoke in sharp tones, "Now, look here, it's nice you came to see my little girl, but you can't be making up stories about helping her get better. We've been going through this for so long now and we've tried all the treatments and drugs that they know. And the doctors here keep testing and testing and they all say there's nothing…" She dropped her head into her hands sobbing. "Oh, please, dear God! Please help. Please help my baby!"

Emmanuel walked closer to the bed. He took Jasmine's hand in his hand. "I can help."

The girl looked into his face. "Who are you?"

"I am Emmanuel."

"My name is Jasmine. It means: a gift from God."

"Yes, child, you are a gift from God."

Jasmine asked, "What does Emmanuel mean?"

Jonny interjected saying, "It means: God is with us."

"I like that name," Jasmine said. The girl looked to her grandmother who turned to Emmanuel and pleaded, "If you can help this beautiful child, then help her. But don't let her be disappointed again. If you can help, then make it so, just make it so." The grandmother echoed her plea, "God, please help my child."

"Just do what he says," Jonny repeated.

The woman nodded in agreement. Emmanuel told her to call for the doctor. After she left the room, Jasmine raised her eyes to Emmanuel and said, "Can you really help me? They say my blood is bad. How can you help me with that?"

Emmanuel answered, "My blood is good. My blood will become your blood."

Jasmine scanned Emmanuel and with a raised eyebrow asked skeptically, "You sure your blood will work inside of me?"

Emmanuel smiled. He revealed his plan, "Take my blood and my life will live in you."

Jasmine listened, understood, and professed, "I believe you, Emmanuel."

The doctor came into the room along with Jasmine's grandmother. Emmanuel told him that he wanted Jasmine to have a blood transfusion using his blood. The doctor rejected the idea saying they had already tried blood transfusions as a therapy. None of them had worked, he stated. Emmanuel responded, "Take the blood I give. My blood is real and the life it brings is true." The doctor looked at Emmanuel with disdain. He persisted vehemently with his objections to the transfusion. The grandmother demanded that the doctor come up with another way to cure Jasmine if he wouldn't try this approach. The doctor reluctantly agreed to perform the procedure.

The doctor asked Emmanuel what blood type he was in order to verify that he would be a match for Jasmine. Emmanuel replied, "I am a universal donor." The doctor left the room confused and frustrated by what he was being asked to do. Nevertheless, he knew there were no other viable treatments and so he ordered the transfusion.

Emmanuel was taken to a surgical room where a nurse prepared him for the transfusion. She pricked his arm with a long needle and drew his blood. After a few minutes, it was over. They tested and verified that Emmanuel's blood was, in fact, a match for Jasmine. It was time for Jasmine to receive the newly drawn blood. They wheeled her in on a table as Emmanuel was leaving the room.

Jasmine reached out her hand to him, "Who sent you to me?"

Emmanuel paused for a moment and said, "My mother told me to help you," as he held her hand in his.

"And you always do what your mother tells you, right?" she said with a grin.

"Don't you?" Emmanuel replied.

Jasmine looked down. "I haven't seen my mother in a long time."

Emmanuel asked, "Why?"

The young girl sighed and said, "One day when I was real little, Mama put my coat and hat on and we drove over to this house that I had never seen before. She sat me on the porch with my suitcase, patted me on the head, and then she turned and walked away." Jasmine raised her head and continued speaking as her eyes grew misty, "I sat there not knowing where I was or what was happening. I wondered if I had done something wrong to Mama. I felt so alone. And then it started to get dark and cold and I started to feel so afraid. I've never been so afraid." She wiped the tears from her eyes. "And then, Grandma came home from work. It was her house, only I didn't know it. She took me in and raised me. I haven't seen Mama since that day."

A nurse came into the room. She lifted up the sleeve of Jasmine's gown. "Sweetie, I'm going to give you a shot to put you to sleep while we do the procedure." She pricked Jasmine's arm with the needle and then wiped the mark and put a bandage over it. "There you go. You'll be asleep in a minute." The nurse looked at Emmanuel and said,

"Sir, you'll have to leave now."

Jasmine gripped Emmanuel's hand. "Emmanuel," she pleaded, "I don't want to be afraid."

Emmanuel placed his other hand gently on her head and said, "You have nothing to fear, my child. God is with you."

Jasmine said softly, "God is with me." She closed her eyes and repeated to herself as she fell to sleep, "God is with me."

Emmanuel leaned over the sleeping girl and whispered, "I am with you."

CHAPTER FIVE

Jonny needed to buy writing supplies and he asked Emmanuel if he would go to the store with him. They walked until they reached a place with the sign 'Petros General Store' above the entrance.

Jonny walked throughout the store picking out his supplies. Then, he went across the store to a brightly lit machine. There was a line of people waiting to use it. He waited in line until it was his turn. When he finally came back to the front of the store to pay for his items, Emmanuel asked him about the machine.

Sheepishly, Jonny said, "That's where you buy the State lottery tickets."

"Why did you buy a lottery ticket?" Emmanuel asked.

"Everyone wants to win the lottery. They say it can change your life."

"How does it change your life?"

"Well, if you win the lottery, you'll get a lot of money."

"And money will change your life?"

Jonny shrugged and said, "That's what they say."

"Let me see your money."

Jonny handed Emmanuel the money. He examined it and asked, "Whose picture is this on the money?"

Jonny looked down at the paper and said, "I think it's the Governor."

"So you buy the lottery ticket so you can win more pictures of the Governor?'

"Yes," replied Jonny.

"And then, after that, will you buy more lottery tickets so you can get even more pictures of the Governor?"

"I guess so," answered Jonny.

"How many pictures of the Governor do you want?"

Jonny stood in confused silence.

"If you had a picture of the Governor in one hand and you had a picture of God in the other, and you could only keep one, which would you keep?"

"The picture of God," Jonny said assertively. "But then what would I do with the Governor's?"

Emmanuel patted the boy on the head and said, "Let the Governor tend to his work and we will tend to God's." Jonny agreed and handed the lottery ticket to Emmanuel.

While they were conversing, a police officer in full uniform came up to the register just ahead of them.

"Good afternoon, Officer Noble. What can I help you with today?" asked the man at the register.

"Hello, Petros. Just these coloring books and crayons for my son."

"Sure thing," Petros replied as he put the items in the bags. Then, with a concerned voice, he asked, "Any news about his operation?"

"No. Nothing new," the officer hung his head before continuing, "The hospital is ready to do it. They think it will cure him. My wife and I want him to have it. But the money—the operation costs so much. I'm working as much overtime as I can. I've sold almost everything we have. I've borrowed as much as I can get. With all that, we still aren't even close to what it will take to get him the operation."

"I know it must be hard for you. I have some money I can lend. Would that help?"

"I'd take the money from you if it would be enough. But the operation costs so much, it wouldn't make any difference. I appreciate your offer to help me but I'm not worthy of anyone's help. But my son, now there is a boy worth saving. Anyone who has been under the roof of our home knows how wonderful he is. He deserves a father who can get the money that will save his life. He deserves better than me."

"Officer, I know it's tough," said Petros, "but don't blame yourself. I'm sure you are doing everything humanly possible."

"But everything humanly possible isn't enough!" the officer exclaimed. "He'll die without the operation. I need help." He dropped his head again and covered his mouth with his hands over his eyes to hide his tears. "God, I need help."

Emmanuel and Jonny were standing nearby and they overheard the officer tell his story about his dying son. Emmanuel looked at Jonny and said, "God's work."

Jonny didn't understand at first. Emmanuel opened his hand and gave Jonny the lottery ticket. Then Jonny knew what Emmanuel wanted him to do. He tapped the police officer on the shoulder.

"Maybe this will help, Sir," he said.

Officer Noble was puzzled by what the boy was handing him. When he figured it out, a small smile creased his face and he replied, "Thank you, young man. That's nice of you to offer. But those things don't work out. They're million-to-one shots. I don't want to create false hope for my son."

Jonny glanced at Emmanuel who tipped his head in encouragement. Jonny turned back and said to the man in the decorated uniform, "It will help. Please take it."

The officer bit his lip and then the smile returned to his face. "Okay," he said. "I'll bring it home to him. He does like watching the television when they spin the lottery balls to get the winning numbers. I guess it doesn't hurt to give him something to look forward to. I heard this is one of the biggest jackpots ever."

The officer paused as he stared at the lottery ticket. "Everything else has failed, but now I have this ticket. One chance for my son to win the money that will pay for the operation to save his life." He looked at Emmanuel and Jonny. "Will your gift make the difference?"

Emmanuel told the man, "Your faith will make the difference."

The officer asked, "Is faith enough?"

Emmanuel said, "The grain of a mustard seed, as small as it is, grows to be abundant in its harvest. So, too, does faith."

"Then I pray that my faith grow as wide as the mustard seed," the officer proclaimed to Emmanuel with his voice shaking, "and that my son lives."

The officer left the store as Petros finished putting Jonny's supplies in a bag. "Here you go," he said as he handed it to Jonny. "I hope you come back. I hope you both come back soon."

Emmanuel and Jonny walked back to the shelter. As they were walking, Jonny asked Emmanuel if the officer's son would get well.

"Faith has made him well already," was Emmanuel's reply.

Jonny nodded his head as they walked silently for a while. Jonny asked Emmanuel about Jona.

"He told us about someone greater that was still to come. He called him the 'Deliverer.' Emmanuel," Jonny asked, "are you the Deliverer?"

"You ask if I am the one of whom Jona spoke?"

"Yes," said Jonny.

"Jona brings joy and hope to the world. And his witness is true. But my witness is not about me, but about the one who has sent me. I do only what the Father commands. I testify to Him and Him alone."

"What does he look like?" Jonny asked.

Emmanuel put his arms around the boy's shoulders. "You can't see his shape or hear his voice but he will know you by your love."

"Emmanuel?" Jonny asked.

"Yes."

"When will you introduce me to your Father?"

Emmanuel stopped. He put both of his arms on the boy's shoulders and said to him, "You know me as I know the Father. There is more that you will learn and more that you will see. In time, all will be revealed to you. And then, the day will come when all the generations to follow will know me by your words."

Jonny took a deep breath.

"Emmanuel?"

"Yes."

"I'm ready to be a witness for you."

Emmanuel rubbed his hand through Jonny's hair.

"In time."

They continued walking. Emmanuel had a question for Jonny. "When you are at the shelter, what do the others say about me?"

"Well, they really like you. They trust you. They like the advice you give them. And they like listening to the stories you tell."

"But who do they think I am?"

Jonny thought for a moment but couldn't come up with an answer.

"Who do you say I am?" asked Emmanuel.

"You," affirmed the boy, "are the Teacher."

CHAPTER SIX

Matilda asked Jonny to bring Emmanuel to their weekly religious lessons to talk to her class. Emmanuel was happy to visit with the young students.

For the first part of the class, she led a discussion of the Scripture reading assigned last week. They talked about the meaning of the words from Second Isaiah, chapter 40, verses 3 through 5:

A voice of one calling:
"In the wilderness prepare
the way for the Lord
make straight in the desert
a highway for our God.
Every valley shall be raised up,
every mountain and hill made low;
the rough ground shall become level,
the rugged places a plain.
And the glory of the Lord will be revealed,
and all people will see it together.
For the mouth of the Lord has spoken."

When they concluded their discussion, she gave them

next week's reading assignment which was a continuation of the Book of Isaiah. This assignment was to read chapter 42 and to reflect on verses 6 and 7. She read aloud those words:

> This is what God the Lord says—
> "I, the Lord, have called you in righteousness;
> I will take hold of your hand.
> I will keep you and will make you
> to be a covenant for the people
> and a light for the Gentiles,
> to open eyes that are blind,
> to free captives from prison
> and to release from the dungeon
> those who sit in darkness."

For the last part of class, she invited Emmanuel to speak with her students. It was a pleasant summer day, and so she suggested they go out into the garden behind the Temple. Matilda asked the children to sit in the grass. She took a chair for herself and brought one to Emmanuel but he found a grassy mound and sat there with his legs crossed and arms folded. The students gathered around him.

"Children," Matilda began. "This is Emmanuel. He is a friend of Jonny's and he has come to talk to us today." She smiled and glanced at Emmanuel as a signal. He smiled back and then looked out at the children. They stared quietly at Emmanuel. After several moments of looking at each other in silence, Matilda interposed, "I have an idea. How about if you take turns asking Emmanuel questions? Would that be alright?" Emmanuel nodded his head in agreement. Immediately, a young girl raised her hand. Matilda acknowledged the girl.

"I have a question," she started. "Why does God let people be poor?"

Emmanuel rubbed his hand over his chin and replied,

"What do you mean by 'poor'?"

"Poor people don't have money and they can't buy things. Some people don't even have enough food to eat," she responded. "Is God mad at them?"

"No, God is not mad at them," he answered. "People may be poor of earthly things or lacking in spirit, but if they believe in God and trust in God, they will be blessed abundantly. And so I say, 'blessed are the poor, they will ascend to heaven'."

Then a boy shot up his hand and asked, "Why are people sad?"

"People do get sad," Emmanuel said. "I get sad, too. It's sad when those you care about are struggling and in pain. Their pain is my pain."

"Will they always be sad?" the boy responded.

"No," Emmanuel answered. "God will comfort them and then they will no longer be troubled or in fear. And so I say to them, 'blessed are those who mourn for their Comforter comes'."

That prompted another child to speak, "My daddy worries a lot. He doesn't say so but I know he feels sad. Will God make him better?"

The inquiring child was wearing leg braces and a set of metal crutches lay at her side. These were the tools of a polio victim.

Emmanuel looked at the child and asked her, "Does your father worry about you?"

"Yes, but I tell him that I'm fine." The girl replied. "I just don't want him to worry so much."

"Your father sounds like a good person. Can you tell him something?" The girl nodded. "Tell him the pain is only temporary and it will go away. Pain only exists in this world. For those who bear their burdens with serenity, new life awaits them. So, I say, 'blessed are those who suffer in peace for the earth will inherit your pain'."

Jasmine raised her hand energetically with a question, "Emmanuel, do good people always go to heaven?"

"Yes," he said, "good people are most welcome in God's kingdom. It is by their goodness we know they are favored by God. And so I say, 'blessed are the good among us, goodness is their reward'. "

Jasmine responded, "So it's good to be good!" The other students laughed.

"Yes," Emmanuel said, "your goodness will come back to you—so be good to others as you would want them to be good to you. And, especially, I say, 'blessed are those who forgive and who show mercy; their kindness will be repaid'. "

"Wonderful!" exclaimed Matilda. "Class, this has been a beautiful day with such beautiful thoughts. Let's have just one more question for Emmanuel before we end our class."

A boy stood up to make himself seen above the other raised hands. "Can you love someone if they don't love you?" he asked. A couple of the girls in the middle row started giggling and one said loudly enough for the others to hear: "He has a crush on someone and I know who it is!" A girl in the front row immediately put both hands over her blushing face.

"Now, class, enough of that. Perhaps we should take another question," Matilda offered.

"No, this is a good question," said Emmanuel. "It's true, someone may not love us at the same time we love them. We prove our love by giving of ourselves, even though we have yet to be loved in return. It is just as God loving us from the beginning though we had not proved our love for him. For love is from God and God is love. And so to the one who loves first, I say, 'blessed are those who love, for their love abides in God and God in them'. "

The boy who asked the question smiled broadly, and the girl in the first row dropped her hands from her face to catch a glance of her not-so-secret admirer.

Matilda stood to end the class. Emmanuel saw at the far end of the second row a young girl with her head hung low who appeared to be in tears. She raised her head slightly, and he beckoned her to come forward. She approached him cautiously and he took her by the hand and sat her on his lap.

"You are sad," he said. She nodded.

"You keep talking about people being good, but what about people who aren't allowed to do good things? God won't want them in heaven."

"Who would that be?" he asked.

"My big brother is in the army. He fights against other people." The little girl dropped her head on Emmanuel's shoulders and began to weep.

"Tell me about your brother," said Emmanuel.

The girl lifted her head and wiped her eyes. "Well," she began, "he's really nice to me and he's funny and when he's home he takes me to the playground and he helps me with my homework. He always helps my mom and dad with fixing up our house, and then one time when the people next door had a fire in their house, he ran in and got them all out safely, even the cat." She choked on her words and continued through her tears asking, "Isn't that good enough for God?"

"Yes, truly, your brother is a man God is pleased with," Emmanuel declared.

"Really? But what about being in the army and fighting in a war?"

"War is bad, isn't it?" the girl again nodded her head in response to Emmanuel's question. "Yes, war is bad," he continued. "There is division across the world; nations rise against nations. Evil people exploit the weaknesses and fears of others. War is bad, but still someone must stand for the meek, the persecuted, the tortured. Still, we must stand for those imperiled and threatened by hate. Still, we stand for the blameless who can't stand for themselves. Your brother stands courageously for those in need and he is prepared to lay down his life for theirs. He is a good shepherd to the innocent lambs and protects them from savage tormenters. He fights so others may live. His is a solemn duty and he accepts that duty at great risk to himself. Is this the man you call your brother?"

The girl straightened up and said proudly, "Yes, that's my brother."

Emmanuel turned his face towards the students and said loudly for all to hear, "Blessed are those who fight to stop evil; an army of angels shepherds them."

The girl wrapped her arms around Emmanuel's neck and held him tightly. Then she went back to her place in the grass among the other children.

Emmanuel stood, looked upon the faces of the children who were gazing back at him, extended his arms and proclaimed:

"Blessed are you children. To you belongs the kingdom of Heaven."

"Thank you so much, Emmanuel," Matilda said. "Now, the students can truly understand the words of the Scriptures from the prophet Isaiah when he wrote in chapter 42: 'Coming to open the eyes of the blind and to free those who sit in darkness'. May I ask one more thing? We've been talking about the power of prayer and connecting with God. Would you lead us?"

Emmanuel nodded and lowered his head with his hands folded. Then he raised his head skyward with his eyes closed.

Our Father.

He opened his eyes and looked out among the children. He spread his arms wide in embrace of them and said, "This is how we pray." He began his prayer:

"Our Father, you reign over all." The children repeated after him. He continued as the children responded in unison after each verse:

"How great you are.

"Your will be done as you command.

"Provide us with our daily need.

"Forgive us as we forgive others.

"Deliver us from the sins and sorrows of the world to your heavenly home.

"You are glory everlasting and we are yours.

"Amen."

Their prayer concluded, the children rose and went to Emmanuel, one by one making their name known to him. To each, he cupped his hand on their forehead and said, "Yes, I know you. Go with the peace I give you."

Matilda thanked Emmanuel for spending time with the students. She left explaining that she had a complicated tax return to complete for a client.

One last student came up to Emmanuel. It was the girl with the metal crutches who had expressed concern about her father. She struggled to make it up to the mound from where Emmanuel had given his sermon to the students. She finally reached Emmanuel and balanced her crutches on the uneven terrain.

"I'm Angela."

"Yes, I know you, Angela" said Emmanuel. "I can see you care for your father very much."

"My daddy is really special. He does everything for us. Since my mom died, he has to work plus take care of me and my twin sisters."

"How old are your sisters?"

"Three years younger than me. They're really neat. They do what they can to help. They can even make their own peanut butter and jelly sandwiches for lunch."

"I'm sure your father appreciates everything you do for each other."

"That's what he always tells us," she replied, "but then I see him staying up late to figure out how to pay the bills. It costs a lot of money for me to keep going to the doctor. He doesn't sleep much. I tell him I'm okay, but..."

"Your father loves you and is concerned about you. Every parent wants the best for their children. No father wants their child to suffer," Emmanuel said.

Angela looked at him and asked, "Does your father

worry?"

Emmanuel thought for a moment before answering, "Every father does."

Emmanuel looked around and saw that everyone else had left. "How are you going to get home?"

"I'll walk. It's not that far, just about six blocks."

"You walk that far with your crutches?"

"I'm used to it."

Emmanuel motioned to Jonny and then asked Angela. "Can we walk with you?"

"Sure," she replied.

The three of them began the walk to Angela's house. It was slow going and a couple of times they had to pause to give Angela time to rest.

After a few blocks, they came upon a couple of boys who were staring up at a tree. They stopped and looked up at the tree. Stuck in the branches was a red ball. One of the boys asked, "Can you reach it, Mister?"

"Let me see," replied Emmanuel as he looked upward. "Actually, I'm not tall enough. Wait, I have an idea." He turned to Angela and said, "Can I have one of those?"

At first, Angela didn't know what he meant. Then she figured it out, bit her lip, and handed Emmanuel one of the crutches. Emmanuel took the crutch and raised it into the tree and knocked the ball free. The ball bounded to the ground and the boys scooped it up and began playing their game again.

"We can go now," Emmanuel said, "but you know, I think I'll leave this here in case their ball gets stuck again. Is that alright?"

Angela glumly nodded her head and walked on with the single crutch.

A block later, they came upon an elderly lady who was limping along the street.

Emmanuel stopped to ask her if they could help. She told them she had twisted her ankle earlier that day and it was causing her a great deal of pain. "Normally, I can walk all day long with no problem, but, with this swollen ankle, I'm having a lot of difficulty."

"I see. I have an idea," Emmanuel said. He looked at Angela. "You don't mind, do you?"

Angela stared at him warily. "I guess not," she finally replied. "Here, ma'am, you can have this." She reluctantly handed the other crutch to the old woman.

"Oh, dear, I couldn't take that from you. You need it more than I do," said the woman as she noticed Angela's leg braces.

"I'm okay," Angela said.

The woman looked at Angela, then at Emmanuel, and said, "If you're sure, well, thank you very much. You're a very sweet girl. Goodbye." She walked away using Angela's crutch.

Emmanuel looked at Angela. "Are you ready to head home?"

Angela turned without comment and faced the long road ahead. She took a step. Then she took another step, and then another. Angela looked around to see if anyone was holding her. No one was. She took another step and then another and continued walking the path home. A wide smile creased her face. She looked at Jonny who had a big grin. They turned on Bethesda Court and got to a house with a large front porch.

"Here is your home," Emmanuel said.

"Yes, this is my home," replied Angela, "but I never told you that."

Emmanuel didn't respond. Angela looked at him with watery eyes and said, "Thank you, Emmanuel."

"Let me help you with one more thing," Emmanuel replied. He took Angela by the hand and guided her to a seat on the porch steps. He opened the locking mechanism on the metal brace. He removed the brace from one leg. He did the same with the other leg. Then he pronounced, "Put these away and walk." He smiled at the girl. "Now go and tell your dad you're home. You don't want him to worry about you."

Angela gazed into the face of the man who had healed her as a tear slid down her cheek.

"Of all the people to help, you chose me. Why?"

"I chose you," Emmanuel answered as he wiped away the tear from Angela's cheek, "because you chose me."

"But I just met you today. When did I choose you?"

"You choose me when you live your life as testimony to my teaching."

Angela wrapped her arms tightly around Emmanuel. Then she walked up the porch steps calling, "Dad! Look at me!" and hurried into her home.

Emmanuel and Jonny walked back to the shelter. Jonny took hold of Emmanuel's hand. After a long while, Jonny said, "People will talk about you when they find out what you did for Angela."

"Then let's keep this a secret," said Emmanuel.

"For how long?" asked Jonny.

"The time is coming."

CHAPTER SEVEN

Nathan and Jamie had gone to town. When they returned later that same evening, Nathan announced that they had discovered what had happened to Jona. He had been taken to a prison in Capital City and was going to trial. They were told that Jona was being accused of inciting a revolt against the government.

"What does that mean?" asked Jonny.

"They are charging him with treason," replied Nathan.

"What will happen then?" responded Jonny.

Nathan and Jamie looked at each other. Nathan paused for a moment and then said, "They've executed people for treason."

Emmanuel went to the front windows overlooking the town. He looked into the darkness, clasped his hands in front of him and bowed his head. After a while, he returned and declared:

"We will go to Capital City."

Nathan, Jamie, and Jonny exchanged glances with each other. Nathan replied, "That's a long trip. And it could be dangerous."

Nathan went on to explain: "The government is threatened by Jona and his popularity among the people.

They don't want to lose control over the people of the State and so they plan to crush any and all signs of rebellion. They're using the government controlled media to cast Jona's supporters as renegades only interested in bringing chaos and ruin to the State."

Nathan said that anyone the government found to be associated with Jona would also come under their scrutiny. As a result, he said it was perilous for them to go see Jona. He stopped and waited for Emmanuel to give his answer.

"We will go to Capital City," he repeated.

They needed supplies for the trip and so they went to the store. After they picked out the food and travel items, they went to pay. Petros greeted them at the cash register.

"It's good to see you, again," he said. "Looks like you are going somewhere."

"Yep," said Jonny excitedly. "We're going to see my friend at Capital City."

"That's a long trip. What's your friend doing there?" Petros asked Jonny.

"He's in jail. He was arrested because of the songs he sings."

Petros asked, "Is your friend Jona, the singer?" Jonny nodded and Petros continued, "I've heard about him. I like him. But I heard the police have been after him for some time. You better be careful." He packed their goods and said, "By the way, Officer Noble's son had his operation last week. He said everything went very well and they expect the boy to be fully cured."

Jonny beamed at Emmanuel.

Petros turned to face Emmanuel and added, "The government office running the lottery sent some agents here to talk to me about the lottery ticket. They seemed confused about how the officer happened to get the winning ticket. They were giving me a hard time about it. After they left, I called my cousin, Markos. He works for the government in the press relations department. He said that the rumor is that there never really was a winning ticket issued at all. The lottery commission was going to announce a winning number in the drawing the following week after it rolled over one more time. For that drawing, they had bribed someone to be a fake winner who would claim the winnings, funnel the money to the government, and then go into hiding. But then Officer Noble came up with the winning ticket, instead. And when he told the press about how the winnings were going to be used on an operation to save his son's life, the government had no choice but to give him the money. They're enraged because they think someone figured out their scheme and beat them to their own scam."

Petros shook his head and continued, "They advertise the lottery as the way to raise money for schoolchildren and then they do this. The government claims to be serving the people but then they prey on them like a den of thieves." He looked to Emmanuel and said, "I didn't tell them about you. Should I have?"

"No. Not yet." Then Emmanuel looked at Petros as if to examine him. He said to him, "Come with us."

Petros' eyes opened wide. He started to stammer and then said, "You know, I would, but my wife is sick with a bad fever and I can't leave her."

"Take me to her," Emmanuel said.

Petros took Emmanuel and Jonny to his upstairs apartment where Petros and his family lived. As they entered their bedroom, they saw Petros' wife lying in bed, her eyes closed, her face flushed with fever and droplets of sweat beading on her forehead. Sitting at her side was a boy sobbing face down on the bedspread. As they drew nearer, she strained to open her eyes and said, "Petros, who is with you?"

Petros started to speak, but Emmanuel interrupted him: "I am Emmanuel," he said as he took her hand in his.

"Emmanuel," she repeated.

"Yes."

"Have you come to take me away?" she asked.

"I've come for your husband. We are going on a trip. I wanted to see you before we go."

She reached out to grasp his hand. She lifted her head off the pillow and whispered, "Petros is a good man, but there are times when he hesitates, when he questions himself. He believes, but then, there are other times when his faith is only the size of a stone."

Emmanuel leaned towards her and said softly, "I will build the church of God on such faith."

Emmanuel placed his hand on the woman's forehead. Then, holding his hand for support, she sat up in her bed. She released him and, of her own accord, rose. The boy lying at her side looked up to her in amazement. Standing, she said with resolve, "Build it with my husband."

Petros looked in wonder at his wife standing before him. The boy who had been sobbing on the bed lifted his head from the bed and saw Emmanuel for the first time. His jaw fell open. He got up and hurried over to him. He engulfed Emmanuel in a hug and cried aloud, "Christos! I knew you would come!"

Petros turned to the others and said in astonishment, "Christos is a Greek word for the messiah. It means 'the Christ.'"

The elated boy released his grip on Emmanuel and turned to Petros, "See Papa, I told you he would come to help Mama. I told you Christos would come!"

Petros put his hand on his son's shoulder. "Yes, Andy," he said. "You were right."

"Yep, I was right, I sure was." Andy said happily.

Petros went to his wife and took her into his arms. "He wants me to go with him."

His wife kissed him and said, "Follow him."

The next morning they boarded the train. Petros and Jamie sat in one row with Nathan and Jonny behind them. They placed their bags on the shelf above. Emmanuel boarded the train empty handed and took a seat across the aisle adjacent to two vacant seats. The train rumbled through the flat terrain that cut through acres of farmland.

Jonny pulled out his journal. Nathan asked, "How is your writing going?"

"There's a lot to write about," the boy replied. He turned to Nathan. "Emmanuel says the world will know him by my witness."

"That's a big responsibility," Nathan said. "Do it well."

Jonny nodded. "How did you meet Emmanuel?" he asked with pen in hand.

Nathan told him about that night in the street. He explained what had happened that had left him begging in bars night after night. He told Jonny how Emmanuel came to his aid against his oppressor and how he lifted him up and took him back to the shelter. Nathan recalled the question Emmanuel asked of him on the street the night he was saved: who do you say I am? He told Jonny that after being with him these months, after seeing him heal Petros' wife, he knew the answer to be just as Andy had declared.

"Emmanuel the Christ," Nathan declared.

They marveled at the sound of the words that had just been uttered. Then they both turned to Emmanuel. He was looking back at them with a tender smile. He tipped his head.

The train came to a stop and several people boarded filling up the open seats. Just as the doors were about to close, a young couple walked aboard. They scanned the train for a place to sit. All the seats were taken except for the two adjacent to Emmanuel. They sat down without comment. The young man took his backpack off and set it on the floor. The young women dropped her large purse to the floor in front of her. It was difficult for her to reach down over her protruding belly. She kicked the purse underneath her and then leaned back into the seat. She sighed uncomfortably as she laid both hands gently atop of her stomach.

The young man placed his cap on the window, leaned

against it, and instantly fell asleep while his girlfriend stared out the window. After a while, she looked around the cabin asking no one in particular, "Is there anything to eat on this train?"

Emmanuel opened his hands that had been folded on his lap. He held up an orange and offered it to her. She responded, "I don't want to take your food from you."

Emmanuel answered, "I have other food."

She thanked him and took the orange from his hand. She pulled out a handkerchief from her pocket and laid it on the top of her stomach. She peeled the orange and placed the peelings on the handkerchief. She split the orange apart and ate a wedge.

"One of the few advantages of being eight months pregnant is having a built-in tabletop," she said with a smile.

"Soon you will forget all your anguish and only know the joy that comes from your child," replied Emmanuel.

"I hope so. It's been a hard road so far, a long, hard road. Sometimes, a lot of times, I worry. I just don't know how this will work out."

"Does worry provide for you?" Emmanuel responded.

"No. But no one else does either," she said annoyed.

"God will."

She twisted her head to look directly at Emmanuel. "God will, what?" she asked.

"God will provide for you."

In an exasperated tone, she said derisively, "Thanks for the orange. I'm going to take a nap," and sharply turned away. When she turned, the orange peels fell from her lap to the floor. She attempted to reach down to grab them, but saw the futility of that and gave up.

They sat in silence. After a lengthy interval, she turned and said in a harsh voice, "Why would you say something like that? Do you know what it's like to be pregnant and not know how you are going to support the baby? Where you're going to live? Don't you know how hard that is?

Tell me: how is God going to take care of my baby? Tell me that."

"Do you believe in God?" Emmanuel asked gently.

"I think so. I mean, I try to believe in God. I used to go to church when I was growing up. I've read the Scriptures. I try to be a good person. But so what? If I thought it would change things, I'd go to Temple or I'd bow to Buddha or I'd go looking for my Karma. But that's not going to help us raise our child. We need a job, I mean, he needs a job. We need money to live on, we need a lot of things that we don't have. If God is going to give all that to me, please tell him: here I am God! Deliver your help now!" Some of the passengers turned their attention to her as she loudly finished her statement.

Emmanuel paused and then said to her, "You worry about what to eat and what clothes to wear and where to live. But isn't life more than that?" He placed his hand gently on her belly. "Does your child worry of such things? Doesn't God provide for her?"

She sighed and hung her head. Then she said, "Yes, I know my baby is safe."

"Your baby is loved, loved by you and loved by God. That's all she knows and that's all she needs," Emmanuel said.

She smiled and nodded her head, "Yes, I know." Then she turned her head and asked Emmanuel, "Wait, my baby is a girl? How do you know that?"

Emmanuel didn't answer. He continued saying, "God made you and God loves you. Each day, every day, God loves you. Place your faith in God's love and the demands of this world will be met."

"It would be awesome to forget all my worries and trust in God's love to care for me, to care for us," she said. "But how do I do find such faith?" She pleaded, "Tell me what I need to know."

"Know God," was Emmanuel's response, "and serve God. You can't treasure God's love while coveting earthly treasures. You need to make a choice."

She paused and hung her head in distress. Then she lifted her eyes and looked to Emmanuel. "Teach me," she pleaded. "Teach me the way to know God."

"I am…" Emmanuel began but then his voice dropped off.

"What? What did you say?"

Emmanuel was silent for a few moments before saying, "I know God. I know the judgments he makes, I know the life he has created, I know the promises he makes. I know his commandments."

Still staring into his face, the young woman said, "I believe you and I believe you know God. I wouldn't be surprised if you knew God better than any man ever has. But how does that help me to know God?"

"Know me and know God," Emmanuel said. "I am," he pronounced, "the way."

At that moment, the train conductor announced the next stop.

"This is where we have to get off," said the woman. She twisted uncomfortably and tapped the young man on the shoulder. He woke groggily and she motioned to pick up their things. He dutifully complied. She turned back to Emmanuel.

"He's really very nice. He'll be a great father. I think he'll be a good husband…a good partner, I mean. We're not actually married. Maybe someday," she said wistfully.

Emmanuel nodded in understanding. Then he took the woman's hand and reached across her to take the man's hand. He placed their hands in his. The young man seemed confused, but didn't object. Emmanuel professed, "As man and woman you are joined together in love and by love you are bound. In God and by his holy design you are one in union. Let no earthly judgment separate what God has joined. Go now in peace. God bless you and God bless your child."

Now joined together, the couple kissed. The train

stopped and they rose to leave. Emmanuel rose, as well, to let them pass.

The woman extended her hand. "I'm Samantha."

"I am Emmanuel," he said as they shook hands.

"I'm so glad to know you, Emmanuel."

CHAPTER EIGHT

They arrived at the downtown train station of Capital City late in the afternoon and hurried over to the jail. When they got to the jail, they were told that visitor's hours had already ended. Moreover, the jail would be closed to visitors for the next two days. They appealed to the prison guard to make an exception given the length of their trip but he did not relent insisting that no visitors would be allowed. The only people allowed inside would be a prisoner's lawyer.

"I'm a lawyer," said Nathan. His traveling companions looked at him in surprise. "Well, I am," he said to them. He reached into his pocket and pulled out a card from his wallet that showed his credentials as a lawyer in the State. The guard skeptically looked at the card and at Nathan.

Petros leaned over to Jamie and whispered, "How did a lawyer end up in a homeless shelter?"

The guard reluctantly agreed to let Nathan in. "But no one else," he barked.

Petros and Jamie looked to Emmanuel who nodded his agreement but Jonny clung to Nathan's arm. Nathan turned to the guard and said, "I need my paralegal to take notes."

The guard objected to the notion, "This boy?"

Nathan looked down at Jonny and said, "Show him."

It took Jonny a moment to comprehend, but then he reached into his back pocket to pull out his journal along with his pen. He displayed his writing tools to the guard and grudgingly, the guard waved them both inside. As they were about to pass through the security gate, Emmanuel asked them to stop. He motioned to Jonny to hand him the journal and the pen. He wrote on a blank page, tore it out from the journal, folded it, and handed it to Jonny.

"Give this to Jona," Emmanuel said.

Jonny stuck the note in his pocket and then he and Nathan went in the jail. A second guard walked them through the dark, damp halls until they got to a cell. There, lying on a cot tapping his fingers against his chest, was Jona. He looked up and smiled at the sight of his young friend. The guard opened the cell and took Nathan and Jonny inside.

"You have fifteen minutes with your lawyer," he commanded.

"Jonny!" welcomed Jona as he embraced the boy. "What are you doing here?"

"We came to see you," Jonny answered.

Nathan extended his hand and said, "I'm Nathan. It's good to meet you."

They shook hands and Jona said, "So, you must be my lawyer."

"Well, actually…," Nathan looked warily to the guard who was still standing with them in the cell.

Jona turned to face the guard and said, "Don't we get to have some privacy?"

The guard responded, "You get whatever we say you get. You think you have rights in here? You're nothing in here. Chief Herold owns you; we own you."

"You don't own me. God owns me—and you can't do anything about that."

"The Chief is your god. You'll learn that lesson the

hard way," the guard threatened.

Jona took a step toward the guard. Nathan put his hand on his arm to hold him back. Jona looked at Nathan and then at Jonny. He went back to his cot, lifted it up, and pulled out a sheet of paper. He gave it to the guard.

"Here," Jona said. "I wrote a song just for you. Give it to Chief Herold, with my regards," he thrust the paper into the guard's chest.

The guard looked down at the words on the paper mumbling as he read:

The sinners are taught,
Deny God love Him not.
Serve the king and his chief,
That's your sole belief.

Whatever you know,
All that you grow.
It's all for the king,
Says the chief and his freaks.

The chief and his freaks
Wield the whip, beat the weak.
They throw down some crumbs,
The lost dine on rot scum.

Whatever you do,
It's not for you.
To the king, pay your rent.
Says the chief satan sent

For souls who must be kept
In a world of sin and regret
They live in dread obedience
To souls who must be kept.

The guard looked at Jona. "I'll give the Chief the song

from the famous singer the people seem to love so much. We'll see well how that goes for you." The guard walked out slamming the cell door behind him.

Jonny looked nervously at Jona. Jona said calmly, "Don't worry about me. I'm fine." Jona and Nathan sat down on the cot and Jonny reclined on the cell floor. "How did you get here?" Jona asked.

"We came on a train," replied Jonny.

"That's a long trip just to see me for a few minutes," Jona answered. Then he reached down and rubbed his hand through Jonny's hair. "But I'm glad you both came."

"It wasn't just us, Jamie came, too. And Petros—he runs the store in town," Jonny said. "And Emmanuel. It was his idea to come and see you." Jonny said. "But they wouldn't let us all in. They said only your lawyer could see you."

"And his paralegal," added Nathan.

"I'm glad to have such an excellent legal staff working for me," Jona responded. Then his voice softened, "But you know there's not much lawyers, or anyone, can do for us. The guard is right. Only the Chief determines what happens around here."

"So what do you do?" Nathan asked.

"Pray," Jona answered, "just pray. And I write songs." He stopped for a moment and then, looking to Nathan, asked, "Tell me about how you know Emmanuel. How did you find him?"

"He found me," stated Nathan. "I was lying under a tree, beaten and thrown out of a bar, with nowhere to go. He picked me up and took me with him to the shelter at Olde Town. Then, he told me to follow him. And I did. Then we saw you at the concert at the river."

"And found Jamie and Jonny," interjected Jona looking at the young boy. "I knew he would take good care of you."

"How did you know?" asked Jonny.

"That night at the concert, I was playing and suddenly I

saw a light shine down from the sky. Then, Emmanuel came out from the light."

Jona paused to consider his words. "For a while, I've believed that someone would come for me, come for us. I've believed that someone would lead us, to deliver us from evil and deliver us from anguish. I started to sing about him. I sang about him before I ever knew him. But then, people started looking to me as someone special. But I'm nothing special, I'm a singer. Then the words poured out of me like rolling waves. The words came to me and the songs came to me. I started playing out in the park, alone among the trees. I sang and people came to listen. I kept singing and people kept coming. I sang about one who will bring the truth to the world. I sang about the one who would bring salvation to those who believed. Then people wondered if I was 'the one' and when I told them that I wasn't, I could see their disappointment. I could see in their faces and hear in their voices the need to know there is something greater than this world. So, I sang more songs filled with the words that came to me. I sang of petrifying our sinning so that we wouldn't be slaves to sin. I sang of purifying our souls so we would be cleansed for the coming of the one who is above all. In the wilderness I sang, and then through the streets I sang. I sang about the one to come who is from heaven and who will show us God, if only we believe. Then, Emmanuel came out from the light. And I knew he was good. I knew he was kind. I knew he would deliver us to a better place. Do you know if…" he reflected for a long time before finally asking the question:

"Is Emmanuel the Deliverer?"

Then they heard the scuffling of footsteps rapidly moving through the hallway. Seconds later, the prison guard stood outside the cell with another uniformed man.

"Chief Herold!" announced the guard.

The Chief bent down and peered through the cell bars. "Isn't it late for visitors?"

"They're his lawyers," the guard retorted.

"Lawyers? The boy? And this haggard looking tramp with the torn and dirty clothes? I think not. So, let me ask you directly, why are you here seeing this rabble-rouser? I would assume intelligent people would keep their distance, lest they be considered accomplices of this criminal."

"Criminals cause injury to blameless people. This man has done no such thing. You have no reason to imprison him and he should be released," rebutted Nathan.

"Ah, I see. Yes, perhaps you are a lawyer. Lawyers like making demands. In this case, as in most cases here, your demands will be completely ignored. But just for my amusement, I'll tell you why he's here. This Jona person is here because he has traveled across the State inciting rebellion against the government. He instructs people to forsake their allegiance to the government, and give it to some mythical deliverer he is witness to. How is one a witness to someone who doesn't exist? Of course he must be insane and, therefore, trouble. But, some of those people believe his nonsense and they've stopped obeying our laws. Some have even stopped paying taxes. What kind of society would we have if people did whatever they wanted, whenever they wanted, without concern for the needs of the government which care for them? It's clear, he's undermining this government and we won't allow that to happen. He will be stopped, one way or another, he will be stopped."

"You don't allow people to be free. Why? What are you afraid of?" said Jona.

"Freedom?" bellowed Herold. "What is freedom? Is it freedom to let people walk aimlessly in starvation and sickness? Is that what you wish for the people you say you are serving?"

"And what do you wish for the people?" retorted Jona. "To coerce their every action? To stifle the liberty God grants them? If you actually cared for the people, their independence wouldn't scare you."

"Independence? Do you really believe these fools could manage for a month on their own? For a week, or for even a day? They would be worse than lost sheep stumbling about the field without the shepherd to guide them," shouted Herold. "You buffoon, don't you know that we are the shepherd who tends to the flock for their own good."

"You aren't their shepherd. You are a tyrant. God is their shepherd. And it is the voice of God they will obey," Jona said.

The Chief bellowed, "Listen to me! This is my voice! Mine is the voice the ignorant buffoons abide by. Where is God's voice? Listen and see if we can hear it."

He stopped speaking and let the echo of his voice drift away. "You see," he said. "It seems only my voice rules in this world."

"Maybe in this world, but God is not of this world. His is the voice I abide by," Jona stated. "His kingdom is the only dominion I seek. And the only truth I know."

"And you will soon know if your God has a place for you there," Herold mocked as he signaled the guard. The guard opened the cell and went in to lead Nathan and Jonny away. As they were about to leave, Herold said, "By the way, I very much enjoyed your song about me. You may be surprised to know that I am going to release it to the people. Fear is a great motivator for compliance. Having Jona, the great baptist and guitarist, depict me as the 'Chief satan sent' will be an effective way to instill terror in the population," he said with a grin. "You should be pleased that your last song will be a big hit."

"He'll write more songs. Let him go and he'll write more songs." Jonny shouted.

"Poor stupid boy, don't you know of the unfortunate accident that will befall your friend during his stay here?" Herold said shaking his head. "Let me spell it out for you. Your friend will never leave here. Never." He motioned to the guard. "Take them away."

The guard grabbed them by the arm and pulled them out. Jonny wrestled his arm away and reached into his pocket. He turned to Jona and said, "Emmanuel told me to give me this to you." He extended his arm to hand him the note. As he did, Herold rushed in and ripped it from his hands.

"I am," he read from the note. "Who is 'I am'? Who is this Emmanuel the boy talks about? Tell me now or I'll leave the boy and this fake lawyer to rot here alongside you."

Jona thought for a moment. He recalled the question he asked just before Herold and his henchman arrived in the cell: Is Emmanuel the Deliverer? He smiled. "It's the answer to a question. It's the answer to life. And, it's the answer you'll never know."

Herold stepped forward and looked down upon Jona his nostrils flaring. "You're so sanctimonious, aren't you? We'll see about that." He turned to the guard yelling, "Get them out of here! I'll deal with the rebel later, once and for all."

The guard took Nathan and Jonny out of the cell and pushed them down the hall. Jonny looked at Jona one last time. Through the bars Jona said, "Tell Emmanuel I'm exiting the stage. It's his show now. My time is past and his time has come."

CHAPTER NINE

Nathan and Jonny left the jail and went to find their friends. Across the street, there was a long line of people stretching for blocks. Nathan asked a passerby why so many people were standing there. She explained that it was a line of hungry people waiting to enter the soup kitchen. Nathan and Jonny crossed the street sensing that's where their companions would be.

The two of them went inside and immediately saw Emmanuel, Jamie, and Petros talking with a man behind a table who was serving soup and bread. Petros waved for them to come over. As they approached, he pulled them aside and told them that the man they were talking to was named Felipe and he ran the soup kitchen. There were hundreds of people who had come for a meal but they were rapidly running out of food. Felipe was trying to cut back on the portions, but there was no way he could serve the people waiting in line.

Emmanuel saw Nathan and Jona and asked, "Did you see Jona?"

Nathan described what happened when Chief Herold arrived. He told him of Herold's threat that Jona would never leave the jail. Emmanuel dropped his head. Jonny reached over and grabbed his hand. Emmanuel looked at the boy sadly.

"I gave him your note," Jonny told Emmanuel. "He was happy when he read it."

Emmanuel said, "I want him to know."

"He's known all along," said Nathan.

Jonny said, "Jona said to give you a message. He said to tell you, 'his time has come.' What did he mean?"

Emmanuel straightened while looking to the building where Jona was being caged. He lifted his head skyward and closed his eyes as if in prayer.

"Is this the day?"

After a few moments, he opened his eyes. His gaze was resolute. He told Jonny and the others, "I have work to do." He asked Felipe if there was anywhere they could buy food to feed the people. Felipe told him he didn't know of any nearby store and the kitchen had no more funds available even if there was.

Emmanuel told them to bring the remaining soup to the kitchen in the back. He told Jonny to bring the baskets of bread to the kitchen, as well. Then he told the others to setup additional serving stations.

Felipe said, "There is no more food in the kitchen. All that's left is in this pot and those baskets. Why should we setup more serving stations if we can't provide more food?"

"I will provide," Emmanuel answered.

Felipe shrugged his shoulders and brought the pot of soup to the kitchen. He returned to the serving station as the line of people stood in need of nourishment. Petros, Nathan, and Jamie each managed a serving station around the room. Jonny went to the kitchen with the remaining bread. Soon, he came out with baskets of bread to each of the four serving stations. He went back to the kitchen and came out with a large pot of soup and delivered it to Felipe. He repeated the trip several times and came back with a large pot of soup each time.

The people in line received their serving of soup and bread and proceeded to sit at the tables to consume their food. The line moved steadily as Jonny kept making his trek to the kitchen and kept returning with soup and bread. After an hour, the line had finally vanished as everyone had been served dinner. The servers looked around the dining hall and saw hundreds of people eating in satisfaction. Emmanuel came out of the kitchen and told his helpers to gather the leftover food and return it to the kitchen. A number of baskets of bread and full pots of soup were returned.

"First, we have no food and then there is enough food is provided to feed hundreds and even after they are all fed, we are still left with abundance," Petros commented incredulously.

Felipe gazed at the man he had only just met and asked, "Who are you?" Emanuel did not answer. He went into the hall to visit with the people. He walked from table to table making himself known. Felipe and his helpers each took soup and bread for themselves and went and sat among the crowd to eat. Petros took an extra serving and brought it to Emmanuel. "Here is yours," he said.

Emmanuel shook his head. "This," he said opening his arms in embrace of the whole assembly, "is how I am nourished."

Emmanuel met a man named Stefan whom he spoke with as he sat eating his food. He told Emmanuel how much he enjoyed his dinner. He said it had been awhile since he had been so well fed. Emmanuel put his arm on Stefan's shoulder and said to him, "There is greater food than this."

"To a starving man, this food is salvation." Stefan said.

"Salvation comes from the bread that brings life everlasting, not from the bread that perishes," Emmanuel stated.

"Tell me how to receive this bread of life and I will give praise endlessly," Stefan replied.

"Believe in the Son whom God has sent and you will never hunger," Emmanuel said.

"Tell me, can a peasant man like me know the Son of God?" appealed Stefan.

"I am my Father's Son," Emmanuel said. "Know me and you know the Father. I am the living bread. Take of this bread and live forever."

"But you're just a man," Stefan said skeptically.

"I am who God has sent to do his will. And his will is simply this: believe in me and you will neither yearn for food nor thirst for drink and you will be raised up on the last day and know everlasting life."

Stefan stared, awestruck, into the face of the man claiming to be God's descendant. He started to speak, but then a commotion at the entrance of the dining hall caught everyone's attention.

A woman and man holding a video camera came into the hall. They stopped one of the people leaving the hall. That person turned and looked around the hall. Then, he lifted his arm and pointed at Emmanuel. The woman and the man hurried towards Emmanuel. Emmanuel started to move to the back exit of the hall but the woman sprinted in her high heels and cut off Emmanuel before he could leave. She smiled and grasped him by the arm. She waved for the cameraman to follow her. From a distance, Emmanuel and the woman could be seen talking in animated fashion. After a few minutes, Emmanuel nodded his head. The woman reached into her purse, brushed her red hair, put a touch of makeup on, and then signaled to the cameraman. The lights from the camera came on as she conducted an interview with Emmanuel.

Felipe, Petros, Nathan, Jamie, and Jonny each went through the entire hall cleaning up the tables. As they were finishing their work, the woman ended her interview with Emmanuel and then she and the cameraman left the building. Emmanuel came over to his friends.

"Our work is done here. Let's return home." he said.

Petros remarked that the last train back home had already left. Felipe said that he lived just a few miles south and they could stay at his home for the night. They arrived there as the dusk fell.

Felipe's home was a small, brick bungalow that sat along the lake. In the back, a fishing boat was docked. Felipe prepared tea which they drank in the front room. He turned on the television and at the beginning of the broadcast, the nightly news began.

"Headlining the news for the day is this exclusive story from our investigative reporter. Judith, tell us about this breaking news from the soup kitchen in downtown Capital City."

The red-haired newswoman who had interviewed Emmanuel in the dining hall appeared on the screen.

"Yes, it was an amazing day here in the downtown soup kitchen. As you know, this kitchen feeds hundreds of hungry people each day. With budget cut-backs from the city government, food supplies have been reduced. This has resulted in long lines and many people not being served. But today, the soup kitchen was visited by a stranger from out of town. Miraculously, the soup kitchen served every single person that had been waiting for their meal.

"I caught up with this do-gooder to get this exclusive interview. Uh, I should note that while we captured the interview with our video camera, for some reason we are having technical difficulties with the visuals. So, we will only be able to play the audio from my interview."

The station then played the audio portion of the interview while the screen on the television displayed a static station logo:

"I'm here at the downtown soup kitchen. For the first time in a long time, the government-run soup kitchen managed to feed all of the hungry people in desperate need of a meal. Apparently, this miracle came about through the efforts of one man. A man named Emmanuel who joins me now. Sir, before I ask you how you were able to feed several hundred people, can I ask you what brought you here to Capital City?"

"I came to see Jona."

"Do you mean Jona, the famous singer who is being held in jail on charges of treason?"

"Yes."

"How do you know Jona?"

"Our mothers were friends a long time ago. I've heard how much his songs were inspiring people and I came to see him."

"You said Jona's songs inspired people. Jona speaks of preparing the way for one greater than him. He sings, 'the Deliverer comes'. Do you know who he refers to?"

"Jona is a shining light and he is a witness to the truth. But there are even greater works than his. It is to those works, accomplished and yet to come, that I bear witness."

"You mean like what you did today to feed the hungry despite reports of the food supply being totally depleted? You gave food to these starving people when there was no food to be had. Is that the reason you came here?"

"My works are not about me. There are those who speak for their own sake and then there are those who speak in praise of another. Of their witness, there is nothing false. I speak to the glory of God. God's will is my will for I am who God has sent."

"God has sent you? For what purpose has God, so you say, sent you?"

"So that all will know God the Father through me."

"Through you? Are you saying that God is discovered through you? But you're just a common man who walked in off the streets."

"Do my words offend you?"

"No, I'm not offended. I'm merely asking a question. Please, wait. Let me ask you one more question. Tell me, tell all of us listening to this interview, how did you feed so many people when the soup kitchen had run out of food? You fed hundreds of starving people when there was no food to be had."

"You believe in my works? Then, believe in me and believe in who sent me."

At that point, the taped interview ended and the news reporter came back on the television screen.

"After my interview, Emmanuel left the building. I should note that as I was leaving the soup kitchen, I was confronted by the assistant to the Chief of Police who questioned me in detail about what I had learned about today's miraculous feeding of the hungry. Apparently, the actions of Emmanuel did not go unnoticed by government officials. I'm not sure what they intend to do, but you only have to consider the plight of Jona to know how strongly they discourage anything that, in their view, undermines their authority. Will this new celebrity named Emmanuel have the same fate as his friend, Jona, imprisoned for months with no apparent hope for freedom? Stay tuned for further exclusive reports. Now, we return to the anchor desk for more news."

"Thank you, Judith, for bringing us that unbelievable story."

Emmanuel went over and turned off the television. He looked around the room and said, "This may be difficult for you. What I say, what I do, can be hard for many to understand. There will be those who hate me and those who persecute me for the words I say and the things I do. And they will hate and persecute those who stand with me. I am here to do God's will and my coming will cause division in the world before it brings peace. If this is not your path, then go."

The others listened in peace. On their behalf, Petros announced to Emmanuel, "Where else would we go? Andy said it first and we believe it now for we have seen with our own eyes: You are the Christ. Our place is with you. With you we stand."

CHAPTER TEN

Late in autumn, the weather in Olde Town had snowed for many days with constant freezing temperatures. Then, the weather improved. A bright, shining sun brought warmth for the first time in a long while. Emmanuel, Jamie, and Jonny went for a walk.

Along the way, they came upon a place of worship that had recently been built. It was called the Second Street Shrine. The Shrine and its congregation were associated with the Community of God religious denomination; the largest church group dedicated to the monotheistic worship of God. Nevertheless, combined with Judaism and some smaller groups, only about one in ten people were avowed believers in God as the supreme deity. Even among these, only a lesser percentage honored their faith in rite and in actions.

Faith, for many people, was rooted in the Scriptures. In Judaism, it was also referred to as the Torah and, to others, simply as the Old Testament. Those that were faithful to the teachings of Scriptures affirmed that God created the world with the words found in the Book of Genesis, "And God said, 'Let there be light,' and there was light." Adam and Eve were known to all the children as the first story of sin. They were taught in the Book of Exodus that God is the father of Abraham, and of Isaac, and of Jacob and of all the people and of all tribes in the world. Moses was revered for the Ten Commandments which were the law of the righteous. They learned from the prophets and read the psalms and pronounced the stories of their idols. The Scriptures dated back to ancient times but they remained the primary vessel of spirituality for God's faithful.

Beyond those sworn to the Scriptures, there were a number of other religions, none of which were prominent. There were scattered groups of Hindus and Buddhists. With increasing types of technology in society, there was a developing formation of people focused on scientific absolutism as the font of truth and wisdom.

The rest of the people were uncertain or uncaring.

This was the world before Emmanuel, but after Adam, after Noah, after Abraham, after Moses, after David, and two thousand years after the crucifixion on the cross of the new born baby Jesus in the massacre of innocents.

Up the long, cement stairway they walked coming upon two large wooden doors. A sign above the doorway read: All are welcome in God's House. They entered.

Inside, they saw crowds of people. Throughout the interior of the Shrine, all the way to the marble altar, there were tables setup that displayed products and merchandise. People were walking from table to table seeking to buy items at whatever price they could negotiate from the various merchants at each one.

After walking through the Shrine for several minutes, Emmanuel asked who the minister was. Someone pointed him out and Emmanuel went to him.

"What is this?" Emmanuel asked the minister.

"I'm sorry. What do you mean?" the minister replied.

"You say this is God's House and yet you treat it as a warehouse for trade."

"Look, we are doing some fundraising for our community. This is the best facility we have. Don't worry, all the money is used to do nice things," the minister said smiling. He turned and completed a transaction with a woman for a porcelain lamp and took her money.

Emmanuel grabbed one end of the table and forcefully tossed it on its side. "God's house is not a marketplace!" The people suddenly hushed as they heard the table crash to the floor and the items spill throughout the Shrine.

"Hey, what are you doing? You can't come in here throwing things around!" the minister bellowed. "I'll call the authorities on you."

"There is no authority but God!" asserted Emmanuel. "You claim to have built this shrine to honor God but instead you repudiate him with your greed and vanity." The people in the Shrine stopped and stared at Emmanuel. He stepped upon the altar.

"Listen to me. It is not God's will to store up treasures of the world. Those will not sustain you. They will wither in the dust and disappear into the wind. Instead, store up treasures in heaven. There, they will not be stolen or lost. For where your treasure is, there is your heart. Keep God in your heart and become a merchant of heaven."

The crowd was speechless. Emmanuel began to leave. The minister asked in bewilderment, "Who are you?"

Emmanuel declared, "I am the gate to this house and salvation comes through me." He marched out with Jamie and Jonny following.

They walked along in silence and headed to the park to walk along the river. The snow was thick and beginning to turn to slush as the sun rose higher in the sky warming the earth even more. Walking alongside the river, they could see sunlight glimmering upon the ice.

Several people were in the park enjoying the warmer weather. They passed one young man sitting on a bench reading a thick book. He nodded pleasantly to them as they walked by.

Jamie and Jonny stopped near the river's edge as Emmanuel walked on. Jonny reached down and placed both hands in the snow. He grabbed a clump of snow, shaped it into a ball, and threw it into the river. The snowball hit on top of the ice and broke apart. He made another snowball and threw it into the river. This one sailed farther than the last and plopped into a patch of water.

After he threw the second snowball, Jonny heard a bark. He turned and saw a small, furry brown dog on the hillside. The dog barked again. Jonny looked around and saw a broken tree branch. He picked it up and tossed it in the direction of the dog. The dog chased after it, placed the branch in his mouth, and then ran to Jonny. Jonny patted the dog on the head, took the branch from his mouth, and tossed it back toward the hill. The dog dutifully ran after it and once again returned to Jonny with his catch. Jonny remembered that he had taken an apple with him for their walk and so he took it out of his pocket, bit off a chunk, and gave it to the dog who quickly ate it.

Jonny gave the dog another bite of his apple. Then, Jonny picked up the tree branch, spun around, and threw it as far as he could. The dog charged after it immediately. Jonny laughed as he saw his new friend in rapid pursuit of the branch. Jonny watched the branch sail through the air and then fall and hit on top of the ice in the river. It slid for several feet before falling off the edge of the ice into open water. Jonny quickly looked back to the dog who was still charging after the branch. Jonny yelled, "Stop!" and started to run after the dog. Jamie grabbed Jonny by his arm to prevent him from going onto the melting ice himself.

The dog swiftly approached the river and then jumped off a snow bank and onto the ice. He started to slide along the ice haplessly. He eventually came to a stop, and sensing something was wrong, began to whimper. His legs started to shake. From the shore line along the river, Jonny and Jamie could hear the ice cracking beneath the feet of the trapped dog. The dog looked towards Jonny with his ears drooping and his tail hanging low.

Then the ice broke.

The dog collapsed into the frigid water. Initially, he popped back up coughing up water. He tried to swim. His legs reached for the ice that was still formed but when he tried to climb on top of it, the ice broke apart. His body, heavy from the ice and water, sank slowly into the river. Jonny tried to break away from Jamie, but Jamie's grip was unrelenting. They both looked fearfully to the river to see if the dog would emerge from the water.

Then, from out of nowhere, they saw Emmanuel reach down into the water and with one hand, pick up the dog by the back of his neck and raise him out of the water. He took the dog into his chest and together they walked to the shore. When they got on land, Jonny took the dog from Emmanuel and placed it against his body to warm him. The dog was still shaking but his eyes were open and his tail was wagging. The young man that they had seen earlier reading a book hurried over to them.

"Did you see that?" he exclaimed. "That guy walked on the water to get that dog! How did he do that? He must be crazy!"

Emmanuel knelt down and rubbed the dog's neck. "Be not afraid. I am with you," he whispered.

Calming down, the young man said, "Here, this will help." He untied a long, blue bandana that was wrapped around his neck and handed it to Jonny. Jonny used the scarf to wipe away the water off the dog's shivering body. Then Jonny reached into his pocket and gave the dog a small piece of his apple, which the dog ate. With tears in his eyes, Jonny looked up at the young man and said, "Thank you." Then he looked to Emmanuel and said, "Thank you, Emmanuel."

Jamie reached down to Jonny and rubbed his head. They headed back to the shelter. The young man, still amazed, expressed his doubts to Emmanuel, "You must have known that there was solid ice on your side, right? I mean, that was still very heroic, but you knew there was ice to walk on, right?"

Emmanuel smiled at him and said, "You were kind to care for the dog as you did. Come and have lunch with us."

The young man paused for a moment before saying, "Well, I'm studying for a final exam, so I'm not sure if I have the time…"

"Follow me," Emmanuel said.

The two walked back to the shelter talking as they went. They got there a few minutes after Jamie, Jonny, and the dog. By that time, the shelter was buzzing with the appearance of their new pet and how he had been saved from drowning. When Emmanuel walked in, the residents stopped talking and regarded him in awe. Emmanuel looked about and saw that he was the center of attention. The dog walked up to him, wearing the blue bandana around his neck, sat on his heels, and lifted his paw. Emmanuel bent down and took the outstretched paw in his hand.

Emmanuel took the young man by the arm and guided him to the dining room. He said, "This is our guest, Toma. He will be joining us for lunch. Nathan, will you make a place for Toma at the table?"

Nathan came over and shook Toma's hand. Jonny sat at the table next to Toma with the dog close by. Jonny asked if he wanted his bandana back but Toma said it looked good on the dog. As the food was brought to the table, the dog tried to hop up on the table.

"Blue," Jonny commanded, "sit."

Once they were all seated, Emmanuel's right hand clasped the hand of Jamie, Jamie clasped Jonny's hand, and Jonny clasped Toma's, and on around the long table until Nathan clasped Emmanuel's left hand completing the bond of fellowship. Emmanuel bowed his head and said, "Father, we thank you for the food which sustains us this day. Yet you offer a greater bounty in the bread you send from heaven that sustains life forever. Those who taste of the living bread will remain in me as I remain in you. This living bread is my body that I lay down so that the world may live. Your have sent your Son to show man the one way home and to raise on the last day all who believe. And I will raise them up on the last day. Amen."

The others responded, "Amen." Some of them began to murmur among themselves. Emmanuel asked, "Why do you whisper? Don't you understand?"

"We understand you are the Christ," Nathan said. "Is there more to know than that?"

"Yes," Emmanuel said. "But greater understanding will come to you in time."

"When?" Nathan asked.

"Soon," replied Emmanuel.

CHAPTER ELEVEN

The advent of winter brought freezing temperatures and heavy snow. Four days after the official start of the season, there was an annual recital being held at Olde Town Square. Several residents of the shelter planned to attend. Jonny saw Emmanuel put on a heavy coat and place a dark wool cap over his head.

"Are you going to the Square for the recital?" the boy asked.

"No," Emmanuel answered. "That's not my place."

"But they are going to tell the story. Don't you want to hear it?"

As they were talking, Jamie came over to listen to their conversation.

"What story is that?" Emmanuel asked.

"The story about the baby who was supposed to be the savior of the world," Jonny responded. "I've never heard it before. Do you know the story?"

Emmanuel grimaced. He closed his eyes.

"Is this the day?"

"I know the story," Emmanuel said solemnly. "Tonight is not for me. You go, though. Jamie can take you."

He looked at Jamie who nodded in response.

Emmanuel said, "Jonny, you should know the story. You should know everything. You are a witness to the truth, remember?"

"I think about it every day," Jonny replied.

"Good," Emmanuel said. "And Jamie is your shield and defender so that you can do what I've asked you to do."

Jonny smiled at his big brother, "I know."

Jamie put his arms around Jonny's shoulder and together they headed to the recital.

"If you're not going to the recital, then why do you have your coat and cap on?" Jonny asked Emmanuel.

"I need to prepare."

Jonny didn't understand Emmanuel's answer but asked, "When will you be back?"

"Soon."

Jonny and Jaime left for Olde Town Square. When they got there, they saw Petros and Andy and greeted them.

A crowd of people had congregated in the Square. In the center, a barren tree was placed. A solitary bell chimed in the silent night to commence the recital.

Each member of the congregation passed somberly by the tree. As they passed, they each put a hand-made decoration on a branch. The last person that passed, a young girl, knelt down and placed an empty baby cradle under the tree. The girl joined a choir who stood waiting, song sheets in hand.

The girl stepped forward from the choir and faced the crowd. She held up her sheet of paper and began to read:

"The story is told from long ago of the babe sent to fulfill the prophecy in Scripture. The words of Isaiah in chapter 7, verse 14, who wrote, 'the Lord shall send a sign; a young woman is with child and will bear a son who shall be named Emmanuel—God is with us.' The story of the baby sent by God to bring faith in the glory of heaven; to bring hope that our lives on earth will be graced by God; and to bring love for each other and love for God. And from these gifts of faith, hope, and love, we know we are all God's children and he will bring us home one day as only God can.

"But the story tells us that this babe born in a manger, our hope of the world, was taken from us by a cruel and evil king. A king who had his mercenaries ravage the land to claim the life of the blessed redeemer. To each babe they found, a sword's fatal thrust was inflicted. All through that savage night, the children were taken victims of the king's fear that his kingdom would fall to the hands of a newborn babe. It is said that among those innocents massacred was the son born in a manger to a young woman graced by God. The child was given the name of Jesus, savior and deliverer.

"Today, we recall the story and we live with the pain. We live with the loss of Jesus. We reflect on what would have been if his life had continued so that his full glory would be revealed to us. What would the world be today if our savior had survived two thousand years ago? How much more joy; how much more progress; how much more prosperity; how much more love? But the newborn king died on the cross and our hope for salvation descended and died. And so we follow him down.

"We gather here now and we ask that one day God's child will come back again to bring light to the world. We pray for God to come to us and show us the way home."

The young girl stepped back into the choir. Their music instructor came forward, stood before the singers, lifted her baton, softly counted the beat, and on cue the choir sang:

**A babe in a manger, a miracle birth
The Prince of Salvation, pure joy from the first.
Then a king oh so evil made war on us all
And claimed as his victim an innocent so small.**

Hallelujah, Hallelujah

Alone on this earth with nowhere to go
Orphaned and broken, oh where is God's home?
What we miss most is what we all lost
When the Savior was born then died on the cross.

So, come back to us
Oh come back to us.
Then raise us up soon
And carry us home.

Hallelujah, Hallelujah

But come back again and show us the way
Give us new hope, raise our souls on this day.
Bring us your love and shine down true light
Choose us and lead us on this silent night.

So, come back to us
Oh come back to us.
Then raise us up soon
And carry us home.

We followed you down
Buried our souls in the ground.
Oh, when will you carry us home?
Oh, oh, when will you carry us home?

The time calls us soon
Our lives almost done.
Our Lord and our Savior
Oh, come back again.

Oh come back again and show us the way
Give us new hope, raise our souls on this day.
Bring us your love and shine down true light
Choose us and lead us on this silent night.

We followed you down
Buried our souls in the ground
Oh, when will you carry us home?
Oh, oh, when will you carry us home?

The song ended and the crowd began to quietly disperse. A few people walked past the tree to glimpse at the empty cradle and reflect on what may have been. Jonny and Jaime headed back to the shelter.

Petros and Andy walked by the tree. As they were walking, Andy asked his father, "Papa, don't they know? They called it a story. It's like they don't know."

"Know what?" replied Petros to the child.

"It's not a story. It's real. Don't they know Emmanuel is real?"

Petros nodded. "Yes, Andy. Emmanuel is real."

"When will they know, Papa? When will the people know that Emmanuel is the Christ?"

"Soon, my son, soon," Petros said.

Petros and Andy left the Square and turned on Emmaus Avenue to head home. As they turned, they passed a man and a woman engaged in conversation.

"Every time I hear that story, it makes me sad. I can't believe someone would be so wicked that they would have little children killed," the woman said

"I know. It's hard to believe."

"But, you know, I wonder if it really would have made a difference. Of course it was terrible for the families who lost their child. But the choir's presentation made it sound like the world would be totally different today if baby Jesus had survived his birth. I'm not sure I understand that. What do you think, Leo?"

"Yes, I know what you're saying, dear. It's difficult to understand how one person could change the world."

"Did Moses change the world?"

The couple turned to see who was eavesdropping on

their conversation. There was a man wearing a heavy coat with a dark wool cap.

"I'm sorry if I startled you," the man said.

"Oh, that's okay," Leo said. "We've just come from the recital and we were talking about the story that was told of Jesus. Were you there for the performance?"

"I came at the end."

"My wife and I were wondering if it would change the lives of people today if Jesus had lived. I mean, it was over two thousand years ago. Even if he had lived a long life, would his life still have meaning this many years later?"

"Did Moses change the world?"

"Well, yes, I suppose he did. At least for a period of time," replied the woman. "Still, you don't see very many people dedicated to his teachings anymore."

"I don't think that many people follow or even know about the Ten Commandments," Leo offered.

Their companion asked, "Moses said, 'God will raise up for you a prophet from among you—listen to him.' Do the people believe that?"

"Yes, I know that verse from Deuteronomy," Leo said. "But if that prophecy was about Jesus, what could he have done so long ago that would be transformative for people today?"

"Show people the way," the man answered.

The woman asked, "The way to where?"

"The way to God."

The couple thought for a few seconds and then the husband said, "Yes. That would change the world. Then, now, and forever."

"Yes, it certainly would," his wife said. "Except Jesus was killed before he had a chance to do that." She looked into the face of the mystery man and asked, "Do you think there will be another who will come and show us the way to God?"

"The time is coming," the man said.

Then he crossed the street and went about his walk.

"Who was that man?" the woman asked.

"I don't know who he is," Leo said, "but I hope he's right. For everyone's sake, I truly hope that he is right."

.

CHAPTER TWELVE

Emmanuel went to see his mother with Jonny at his side. The nurse saw him, abruptly rose up from her chair, and asked him, "Can I speak with you, please?" Emmanuel lifted his arm with his palm outstretched to indicate he couldn't speak with her now.

He continued on to see his mother passing by Mr. Simon's room. He looked to see if the old man was there. Mr. Simon looked back at Emmanuel and, as he did the last time, turned away.

When he entered the room, he saw the doctor who was attending to his mother. His mother lay still in her bed, her eyes staring at the window. The doctor went to Emmanuel and spoke in quiet tones.

"I'm Dr. Lucas. I'm a new physician here. Are you a relative?"

"I'm Emmanuel, her son."

"I see. I need to inform you about the results of my examination. She hasn't been eating well and her vital signs are not very good. She's been lapsing in and out of consciousness. When she is awake, her speech is not very clear. She can barely complete a sentence. She doesn't even know her name."

"Mary," said Emmanuel.

"Yes, well, she hasn't been able to get of bed and so her muscles have atrophied. The nurse says she doesn't sleep much. She tosses and turns and calls out randomly throughout the night. I'll prescribe sedatives to keep her calm but I'm afraid there isn't much else we can do. She will continue to digress until…"

"My son."

They turned at the sound to see Emmanuel's mother looking at her son. Emmanuel came to the bed and placed his hand on his mother's and leaned over to kiss her cheek.

"Mother," he said smiling.

She smiled back at him and then, raising her head off the pillow slightly to look about the room, said, "Who is that boy?"

Emmanuel answered, "That's Jonny. He lives with us in our home."

"Uh-huh. Who's that?" she said pointing her gnarled finger to the doctor.

"He's just visiting," replied Emmanuel.

"Uh-huh. Invite him to dinner?"

Emmanuel looked to the doctor who replied to her invitation, "Thank you for the offer, but I need to be going now."

Dr. Lucas turned to leave the room. Then, she asked, "Have I told you about the dream?"

The doctor looked at her quizzically and then to Emmanuel who remained silent. He walked back towards his patient. "No, you haven't told me about the dream."

"Let me tell you."

She took Dr. Lucas' hand in hers and told him about her dream:

"It was a time long ago. I was young. I was living with my parents. And then they went away and left me. One night, I came home and went to my bedroom and lay on my bed. Then, the dream came upon me. I saw a vision above me; a body glistening and flowing through the sky. I covered my eyes, for I was afraid, but then a voice said: 'Fear not, for I bring you great joy. You, of all women, are most favored. On this night, you will conceive a child, as God intends.' I was confused and asked how could this be and the voice told me to remember what the prophets said, 'The young woman will bear a child and call him Emmanuel—God is with us.' And then when my parents came back, I told them of my dream. But they didn't understand. Night after night, they would argue with me, but I never doubted because I knew it was God's will. They finally sent me away to live in a place that they said would be better for a mother. And after a few months there, I was rushed to the hospital and all through the night I saw visions of bodies in white garments floating above me, speaking and moving about and I remember crying in pain. But then, at last, they showed me the child, my child. And I heard the voice saying, 'Here is delivered your son, glory to God.' And his hair is dark and his eyes are wide and he is looking at me as I am looking at him, and I know this is what God has divined and I know this is God's Son. And I am so filled with joy, I sing the song."

The doctor looked upon the woman who had only minutes earlier been decrepit in body and demented in mind. He listened as Mary sang her song:

My soul magnifies the Lord, our King,
With the Son that lives inside of me.
I am blessed by God for Him I sing.

God delivers grace and glory
To servants of simple circumstance.
Trust in the Lord and set yourself free.

Divine wisdom confers the commandments:
Love is our purpose, redemption our fight;
Forsake fortune, fame, vain indulgence.

God proclaims through the golden light,
Be honest, helping, kind and true.
He is our Savior, we are dear in his sight.

Be not afraid, God's love renews.
Tears and troubles desist and die,
True life begins when heaven welcomes you.

With the Holy One, Lord I do magnify.

She finished and looked up to Emmanuel. She repeated the words, "With the Holy One, Lord I do magnify."

Dr. Lucas stood incredulous at what he had just heard. He tore up the prescription he had written for her as she continued to tell him more of the miracle birth.

The nurse saw Emmanuel leaving his mother's room. Again, she asked to speak to him.

This time, Emmanuel turned to her and said, "Martha, tell me why you are distressed."

"It's my sister. She's been here before to visit. Now, she is in terrible trouble. Please help her, if it's not already too late." Martha took a handkerchief and wiped away her tears. "I know you can help her. Will you help her?"

"What do you ask?" Emmanuel said.

"Please go to her. She is suffering. She needs help. You are the only person she can trust, the only one she will believe."

"You speak of her belief. What do you believe?" he asked.

"I have heard your words and I have seen your works," Martha acknowledged.

"I do what God has willed me to do."

"I know," the nurse answered.

"And his will is that those who believe in me will not die but have life everlasting," Emmanuel said. "Martha, do you believe?"

"Yes, Emmanuel," Martha confirmed. "I believe."

"Tell me where she is."

Martha told him where her sister was and what was happening. Emmanuel grew stern and brusquely turned to leave.

Dr. Lucas grabbed him by the arm as he walked by.

"I've never seen anything like that in my entire life," the doctor told Emmanuel. "I thought her dementia was in its final stages. But that story, how vividly she described her dream, it was as eloquent as anything I've ever heard. Then the song, how beautifully she sang. She remembered every verse, every word, every rhyme. It was inspiring. And she said it all with such deep conviction; it was as if she had just experienced it. She said that you," he paused, "she said you are…"

"I must go," Emmanuel stated.

"Go? But why? Is something wrong?"

"I have work to do."

"But I want to hear your account of all that has transpired."

Emmanuel freed himself from the physician's grasp, stared into his eyes, and declared:

"I come to rage fire on the world and it's time for it to blaze."

Emmanuel left the shelter. Toma was walking along the street when he saw Emmanuel. Emmanuel was fixed on reaching his destination and did not see Toma. Toma stretched out his arm for Emmanuel.

"Teacher, where are you going?"

Emmanuel's eyes glistened. "I go to save the innocent from the vicars of death," he vowed.

Toma saw the resolve of his counselor and declared, "I'll go with you. Death has no quarter in the presence of the Christ."

Together, they went to the address given them by Martha. They walked through the door with a sign reading: Planned Parenting Clinic. When they entered, they saw several women, most young, some very young, sitting in waiting areas. Some were with friends, but others were all alone. The carpet was stained, the walls showed cracks, and a stench filled the building. From behind a glass-enclosed desk, a receptionist slid the window open slightly and said to them, "Are you here to pick up a patient?"

Emmanuel said, "I'm here to see Magdalena."

The woman responded tersely, "Magdalena is working and cannot be disturbed."

Emmanuel ignored her command and pushed through a set of double-doors.

"Stop right now! No one is allowed back there!" the women at the front desk shouted. Emmanuel marched through the doors and down a wide, barren hallway. He went by a room that had a sign reading: Surgical Suite. In the room was a woman lying on a table groaning in agony with blood dripping down from between her legs. A man wearing a long, gray, blood-spattered robe and holding an elongated set of scissors saw Emmanuel and yelled at him, "Hey, what are you doing here? Get out now before I call the police!"

Emmanuel proceeded down the hallway undeterred while Toma stayed back to protect his passage.

From behind a closed door, Emmanuel heard someone crying. He opened the door and saw a woman wearing a nurse's uniform with her head hung low, tears streaming down her face. She was standing and looking down upon a metal cart. On the cart, lay a white, cloth blanket.

"Magdalena," Emmanuel said as he walked inside. She refused to take her eyes off the blanket. "Magdalena, I am Emmanuel."

She slowly lifted her head to face him. "Emmanuel? You are the one Martha told me about."

"I'm here," Emmanuel said.

She shook her head wildly and cried out, "It's too late to help." She pounded her fists against his chest and repeated, "You're too late!" Emmanuel grabbed her hands and pulled her into his arms. She sobbed uncontrollably. "I didn't know, I didn't know. I am a sinner. I'm sorry, I'm so sorry."

"Sin is with all people," Emmanuel stated. "I have not come to judge you."

As Emmanuel held her in his arms, his gaze moved to the blanket on the table. He stared in disbelief at what lay in the blanket.

A baby.

He released Magdalena and lowered his head.

"I didn't know," Magdalena said once more. "When they told me what this job was. I didn't know they were babies. I don't know what I thought they were but I didn't think they were babies. I've been working here for a week and so many of them, so many of them look like babies. And then, he…we…just kill them. He uses long scissors and goes inside the women and…But, today, this one…" Magdalena looked at the blanket with the tiny, motionless body inside, "This one was breathing after they cut him out. I told the doctor, 'He's alive, we need to help him' and the doctor said, 'No, that's not what we do.'"

Magdalena looked at Emmanuel. "Then he told me to throw it away! 'Throw it away,' he ordered me." Her hands trembled as she continued, "How could I throw a child away? I couldn't…I wouldn't. So I put the boy in a blanket and brought him here and I've stayed with him ever since. For a while he kept breathing. And then, he stopped," she said choking on her words.

"He's not breathing," she continued. "But now I don't know what to do. He said to throw it away, but I won't. I won't throw it away. It's a baby."

Emmanuel kept his gaze concentrated on the new born babe. When he finally lifted his face, his eyes were welled up with tears. He looked upward. Extending his arms with palms outstretched, he prayed:

"This is the day I ask your glory to be revealed in me."

Emmanuel placed a single finger on the baby's chest. He pushed gently on it and proclaimed aloud, "Come forth, child."

A rush of air blew through the baby. Then the baby's arms jerked and his hands clenched. Magdalena saw the infant move. She placed her hands over her mouth in astonishment. The baby continued to move and toss about.

Magdalena walked hurriedly to a cabinet and found a small eye dropper. She twisted off the rubber top and poured water into it. She replaced the top and came over to the baby and placed it tenderly into his mouth. She squeezed the top ever so lightly to release a drop of water into the baby's mouth. The baby took both of his hands and grasped the plastic dropper as Magdalena nursed him to health.

Magdalena smiled blissfully. She exclaimed, "Thank you, Emmanuel. You brought him back to life."

"It was you who refused to let him die. This baby is yours now; yours to love and yours to name. He is blessed by God the Father. Teach him to live according to God's will."

"Yes, I will. I will teach him to serve God." She beheld Emmanuel. "And I will raise him to listen to your words and to follow your way."

Magdalena picked up the baby in the blanket and held him to her chest.

"My little brother was a very good boy," she said. "He died years ago of an illness. I want my son to be like him. I want my son to be like Lazarus."

She and Emmanuel walked out of the room and down the hall to the waiting area with Toma following behind. The women sitting there saw Magdalena with the baby safely in her arms.

One by one, the women came to view the child who was to have been shredded and discarded. One pregnant woman conveyed the revelation they all experienced, "Oh, my God," she said, "I didn't know. It's a real baby. They made it sound like it wasn't real. But see how he looks, and how he moves, and how he sounds. It is a baby, a beautiful little baby boy."

One by one, the mothers rose and followed Magdalena out of the clinic with their babies still alive, still loved, protected inside them.

CHAPTER THIRTEEN

The sound of loud sirens raged through the stillness of the cold night. Speeding down the streets with lights flashing, the police cars raced by the shelter. People from neighboring buildings peered out of their windows to find the cause of the disruption. A few blocks away, the police cars came to a halt and officers began to encircle the area. Curious on-lookers made their way to the site of the commotion to get a closer view.

In short order, two policemen had arrested a teenaged boy, handcuffed him, and dragged him to their squad car. The teenager struggled with his captors until a heavy-set officer with a thick mustache grabbed him by the back of his hair and slammed the boy's head into the roof of the car. Blue barked at the brutality and tried to jump at the officer but Jonny held firm to the leash that was now part of every trip the dog made. The policeman yelled at Jonny to keep the dog away or he would shoot it. Jonny gripped the leash tightly with both hands.

Youngsters started coming out of the building hurriedly putting on their coats and hats as they came out into the freezing weather. An adult acting as a supervisor clapped his hands sharply and made emphatic gestures with his arms to direct the boys and girls to a secure area. After a few minutes, the adult came over to the squad car where the teenager was being held and spoke with the arresting officers.

"I don't know what got into him. All of a sudden, he just started running through the residence hall breaking all the windows. We've had trouble with him before, but not so much lately and never like this."

"Are all the students out of their rooms?" asked one officer who looked familiar to Jonny.

"Yes, all thirty-five students are accounted for. Of course, with the windows broken and this extreme cold, we will have to find another place for them to spend the night."

"Don't they have families nearby you can contact?"

"A few do but most don't. We're the only school for the deaf in the area and many families live far away. I've been the headmaster here since the school opened up six years ago and most of the kids are full-time residents."

The officer asked the headmaster about previous incidences of vandalism or violence.

"We have issues here," he explained. "Being deaf and with little family support, some of these kids do have behavioral problems. But, they are supportive of each other because they know they understand one another better than anyone else does. That is what binds them together." He shook his head from side to side. "I just don't know what got into him. As I said, he's had difficulties before but they were minor. He came here two years ago. He had gotten into a car accident and had lost his hearing from the extreme force of the airbags. His hands were also mangled in the crash which has hampered his ability to use sign language. And, as it often happens, once someone loses their hearing, their speech goes, as well. Now, he can only grunt some sounds."

The headmaster continued his conversation with the police officers, "His parents tried to keep him at home but there was no way he could be taught at the local schools, and he couldn't maintain any friendships. So they brought him to our school. Even here, it's been a very tough adjustment for him in communicating with the others since he became deaf later in life. But still, he's a good kid, especially given what he has gone though. It doesn't make any sense."

"We'll bring him to jail and keep him there overnight at least."

"Jail? Isn't there somewhere else you can take him? That's not a place for this boy," the headmaster said.

"This is a crime and jail is where we take criminals," was the response.

"But how will he communicate with anyone? He won't know what is happening. He'll be frightened and alone."

"Then send someone over who can communicate with him."

The headmaster replied, "We have dozens of kids we have to find safe places for tonight. Who can we send?"

"Send me."

The policemen and the headmaster turned their heads. One of the policemen lifted his flashlight to look into the face of the man who voiced the words.

"Do I know you?" he said after a brief pause.

"How is your son?" came the reply.

Officer Noble lowered the flashlight. "It's you." He took a step closer and reached out his hand to Emmanuel. "It's good to see you again. My boy is doing great now that he's had the operation. The money from the lottery ticket you gave me covered everything."

"You got the winning lottery ticket from this guy?" interrupted the mustachioed officer.

Officer Noble ignored the comment. "You know, with our experience at the hospital, we have gotten to know several children with serious illnesses. We've decided, my wife and my son, to use the rest of the lottery winnings to get the best medical treatment for all of them, too."

"Your good works are witness to your kindness and compassion," Emmanuel said.

"I feel very fortunate to be able to help those kids, to help my kid." He smiled. "But somehow I think I have you to thank for all of this."

"I only do what I've been sent to do."

The heavy-set cop interrupted, "Alright, that's enough gabbing. Let's go. We gotta get this punk to the jail," and then he plopped himself into the front passenger's seat of the squad car.

The other officer responded dutifully, "Okay, Sarge." He took the boy by the arm to place him into the backseat.

"Let me talk to the boy," asked Emmanuel.

"Look, it's late, it's cold. I know you want to help but the kid was caught red-handed breaking the windows to the building where all the students slept. There's not much to talk about. Plus, he doesn't seem to be able to communicate with anyone."

"Let me talk to him," Emmanuel repeated.

The officer looked at the boy who was still groggy from having been slammed into the roof of the car. He guided him away from the car.

"Hey, what do you think you're doing?" yelled the sergeant from the car.

"Just five minutes," the junior officer responded.

The handcuffed boy faced his intercessor. Emmanuel placed his thumb over his clenched fingers and raised his hand up and down, expressing the boy's name in sign language.

The headmaster asked with surprise, "Say, how do you know the sign-name for Shiloh?"

Next, Emmanuel brought his right fist to his chest with his pinky finger extended and followed by taking the same hand, clenched with the thumb outside the fingers, and moved the fist away.

"I am," repeated the headmaster orally.

He continued by extended his arm, pointing with his

index finger, and then brought it back towards his body in a downward arc.

"God."

He knocked both fists together and then took the right hand touching the right shoulder and swung it across his chest to touch the left shoulder."

"With us," the headmaster translated. "I am God with us?" the headmaster summarized without understanding.

"Emmanuel." They looked at Jonny. "His name is Emmanuel. It means, 'God is with us'."

Emmanuel remained focused on Shiloh. He cupped his right hand around his ear and pointed to himself.

"Listen to me," the headmaster translated. Emmanuel followed with a series of signs to which the headmaster interpreted, "He asked Shiloh to tell him what happened. He won't get a response, though. Shiloh is not good at signing."

Shiloh opened his mouth to speak but only a muffled grunt came out. He bit his lip in frustration. He jiggled his hands but they were trapped in the handcuffs. Emmanuel looked to the officer for assistance. Knowingly, the officer nodded and took out his keys. He unlocked the handcuffs.

Emmanuel took the boy's hands in his. Then he placed his hand on Shiloh's lips.

The boy straightened. Methodically, he signed:

"I"

Then he brushed his hand by his nose:

"smell"

And then he poured one hand into the other to indicate:

"gas."

Alarmed, the headmaster exclaimed, "Oh, dear God—you smelled gas?" Shiloh nodded his head.

The officer quickly ran over to his the other policemen at the scene. "Hey, there might be a gas leak in there. Let's clear these kids out of here now!" They acted in unison to gather all the children and move them far away from the building. Once the building was emptied, they had two firemen examine the facility for gas leaks. After several minutes, they came out, pulled off their masks, and reported that there were very high levels of natural gas throughout. They explained that a leak was found in the line to one of the furnaces. Then one of the fireman said, "If that kid hadn't broke the windows to let the gas escape, a small spark could have caused a massive explosion. That young man kept a lot of people safe from harm tonight."

The students gathered together. The headmaster signed to them how Shiloh had smelled the gas in the building and broke the windows to let the gas escape so everyone could get out before an explosion could occur. He pointed to Shiloh, brought his hand to his forehead, pushed his thumb and fingers together and extended both arms with fists clenched:

"Hero."

The students clapped and surrounded Shiloh to hug him and pat him on the back. Shiloh smiled jubilantly. When they had finished thanking him, Shiloh signed to them:

"I didn't know what else to do when I smelled gas. I wouldn't let anything bad happen to you. You are my friends, my family. This is my home."

They all viewed him with amazement. He had never signed so fluently before. The headmaster faced Shiloh and asked him how he was able to sign so well now. Shiloh gave his witness to Emmanuel:

"Emmanuel touched me. I was silent but now I speak."

They all turned to Emmanuel. Emmanuel said to the headmaster, "Let's get the children to our shelter down the street. We can care for them there."

While they prepared to take the children, one deaf youngster began to bang on the bass drum that he took out of the building when they were told to escape. The booming bass sound could be heard by those who retained some level of hearing. Others could discern the beat from the vibration emanating from the drum. As they gathered around Shiloh, the young man started banging on the drum the familiar beat of their school's victory chant. Those with voices sang out and the others signed in rhythm to the beat of the drum:

**We've won
Whenever we're one
We've won
When right has been done**

**Our dream: one team
Our choice: one voice
Brothers! Sisters!
We're family first**

**We're one
We've won
We're one**

Meanwhile, alone in the squad car, the police sergeant hurriedly placed a call to Capital City.

"Yea, connect me to Chief Herold. I don't care how late it is, just do it.

"Chief? Yea, remember you told us to keep a look out for the guy who went to the Capital and fed all those people in the soup line? Well, I think I found him. He's downstate in Olde Towne…I don't know why he would be here, either, but he is. And you won't believe what he did tonight. Not only that, but remember how you said nobody could figure out how the winning lottery ticket happened? Well, this guy was in on that, too. I can arrest him right now on some phony charges so we can work him over back at the jail…No? Okay, but you should see how these people here adore him. First, that singer Jona got them all righteous and now this Emmanuel character is here working miracles. If you want to keep everything under control, you better do something about this guy.

"These people worship him."

CHAPTER FOURTEEN

Soon the days became longer and the weather warmed. Lazarus grew bigger and stronger and Magdalena brought her baby boy to visit friends at the shelter. She brought a bottle of vintage wine and a wheel of aged cheese to give as a gift to Emmanuel.

The door to the shelter opened and a red-headed woman walked in from the outside.

"I'm Judith," she said smiling. "I'm with the news station in Capital City. I interviewed Emmanuel when he fed all those people at the soup kitchen."

Nathan and Jamie, who were visiting with Lazarus, looked at her in silence.

"Well, anyway," she continued, "I received a tip that Emmanuel lives here." She surveyed the shelter. "I find it hard to believe that someone like that would live here but that's what I was told. So, is he here?"

Nathan and Jamie glanced at each other but remained silent.

"He is here, I take it. Can you tell him I'd very much like to do another interview with him? We received great feedback from the last one. It was one of our best rated segments ever. My editor told me if I can get another interview, I can get promoted," she explained with a broad smile. "Plus, he said I would be up for a thirty percent raise, which I could really use." Again, her comments were met with no response. She looked over to Magdalena who was holding Lazarus and said dryly, "A little baby, how nice." She saw the gift basket that Magdalena had brought for Emmanuel. She picked up the bottle and examined it. "This is a very expensive bottle of wine. I'm surprised a homeless shelter would be indulging in such extravagant gifts." She placed the bottle down and in exasperation, once again, asked to see Emmanuel: "Look, I'm just here to help. Isn't it better if more people know about this amazing man? Why keep him a secret?"

Jamie turned to Nathan and nodded. Nathan went to the room upstairs to see Emmanuel.

"Thank you," Judith said. She noticed Jonny sitting at a nearby table writing in his journal. "Hello, young man. What are you writing about?"

Jonny looked up in surprise. He answered the reporter's question: "My project."

"And what is your project about?"

"I write what happens so people will know the truth."

"The truth about what?"

"The truth about Emmanuel."

She pulled out a chair next to Jonny and sat in it. "You've written down in this journal all the things that have happened with Emmanuel?" Jonny nodded. "Can I see your journal?" she said as her hand reached over to the book. Jonny pulled it from her reach. She leaned back in her chair and said, "I see. Well, how about if you tell me some stories from your journal? I would love to hear all the wonderful things you've written about Emmanuel."

Jonny thought a moment and then said, "Well, there was this time…"

Judith interrupted him, "Just a second. I have a little cold and I want to get my handkerchief out." She reached into her purse under the table and after a few seconds took out a handkerchief and then placed it on the table pushing it near Jonny. Jonny thought he heard a "click" noise but disregarded it. She smiled and said to Jonny, "Please go ahead. Tell me everything. I can't wait to hear it all."

Jonny told Judith the stories that he had written in his journal. Occasionally, she would ask questions but mostly she listened to Jonny as he told the truth of what he had witnessed. When they were finished, she cupped the handkerchief in her hand and gently put it back into her purse. Again, there was a "click" noise.

"That was incredible, Jonny. Thank you for sharing those stories with me," she said. "I'm sure I'll never forget it." She patted Jonny on the head and stood up. "Has he come down yet?" she asked.

"No," said Nathan. "He's not coming down."

"But why? I've made this long trip to this awful place just to see him. He must talk to me. What will I tell my editor?"

"He said to do what you intend to."

Her jaw dropped in disbelief. She tried to speak but was unable. She turned in a huff and marched off. At the same time, the door flew open and Toma came into the shelter. He bumped into the reporter and her purse fell to the ground dropping her belongings. Toma apologized and reached down to help put pick up her items. He reached for a small black device wrapped in her handkerchief, but she slapped his hand away and picked it up herself. They rose and Toma apologized again.

"I'm sorry." He turned to his friends. "I was at the post office and there was a delivery to the shelter so I picked it up for you. Here," he said as he handed it to Nathan.

Nathan opened it and pulled out a tape. Attached to the tape was a note. He read the note out loud:

"I visited Jona. He said he is doing fine but he didn't look good to me. But he asked about you all and he gave me this tape. He said it's a song. He wants you to have it. He wants everyone to hear it. Don't ask how he made it, people could get in big trouble, but I was glad to sneak it out of that rat-hole. Felipe told me where you are. Best regards, your friend, Stefan."

"So, you have friends that are aiding and abetting a jailed criminal? We'll see what the authorities think about that!" Judith shouted. She exited the shelter with the door slamming firmly behind her.

The others ignored Judith as she stomped away. They were focused on the tape and the new song from Jona. Since the shelter didn't possess a tape player, Toma said he would ask a friend who was a DJ at the college radio station to play it on the air so everyone at the shelter could hear it.

Toma went to the station the next day and his friend agreed to play the song later that same evening. Everyone at the shelter gathered around the radio in the main room. Emmanuel stood gazing out the window. Finally, the DJ announced the song.

"We have a sensational exclusive for you tonight. We have a brand new song from Jona to play for the very first time. Yes, Jona, locked up in jail in Capital City, has somehow managed to make this new song and it has found its way to us. I listened to it earlier today and I think you're going to love it as much as I do. For the first time ever, here is 'Run to the Light' by Jona."

Trapped in this cell on a hot summer's night.
Got to get free so I can run to the light.
Time to baptize so I can get these souls clean,
Show them way, just like they dream.

Jump out of this hell, hey-hey, free me!
Let's run to the Light.
I'll show you the way,
I'm not going to hide.

Cause I'm trying, trying for God's love

And I'm dying, dying for God's love

Time to check out, escape all the hate.
This is my call: prepare the way.
Emmanuel lives, God is with us.
The Deliverer shouts: Come into my house.

Jump out of this hell, hey-hey, free me!
Let's run to the Light.
I'll show you the way,
I'm not going to hide.

Cause I'm trying, trying for God's love
And I'm dying, dying for God's love

The song ended and the residents in the shelter applauded. When their applause faded there was a strange silence on the radio. There was background noise that couldn't be understood. Faintly, a voice on the radio was heard saying, "Are you sure? Maybe the report is wrong?" Then more silence. The listeners in the room started to shift uncomfortably and moved closer to the radio to hear. Finally, the announcer came back on:

"Ladies and Gentleman, I have just received a breaking news story. This comes from Capital City. It is being reported that Jona has been shot.

"The shooting occurred in the jail where Jona has been held for many months. The report states that he was shot in the head by police. It is not known what provoked the shooting but the police there are under the command of Chief Herold." The voice paused and struggled with his words. "Those who listen to this radio station, know Jona well by his energizing music and by his powerful message. Jona is the man who has been an inspiration for many; the man who stepped into the void to cleanse people of their wrongs and to baptize people in God's name. Jona is the man who came to prepare the way for one greater than he and who sang about it in the song, 'the Deliverer comes'."

He paused once more choking over his tears and then concluded his statement:

"Jona has been killed."

CHAPTER FIFTEEN

In the days that followed Jona's death, there were rampant acts of rebellion in the streets. The official press release said that Jona had tried to escape from jail and was shot after he attacked the guards. Few people believed that.

Now a martyr, Jona became an even bigger story to the people. The new song that debuted the day he was killed became the theme for the people to fight back against the oppression of the government. All day long, radios would blare, "Jump out of this hell, hey hey, free me!" to reflect their own rejection of the world in which they lived. The music stores quickly sold out all of his songs. People began to greet each other with the phrase, "the Deliverer comes!"

As their indignation against the central authorities grew, their obedience to the law diminished. Government tax bills were returned unopened, curfews were ignored, and politicians were publicly ridiculed. The head of the State, Governor Platt, went on television to denounce those who, he said, were promoting anarchy. At the same time, he ordered the police force to make examples of anyone thought to be breaking the law. Hundreds of citizens were arrested and brought to jail. Several people were found dead from gunshots after confrontations with the police.

Markos told Petros what he had heard in the interiors of the Governor's mansion as he was preparing various government statements. The growing lawlessness in the cities caused some to believe that another strategy to quell the rebellion was needed or else the State would begin to disintegrate. They talked about the provocation caused by Jona and that his death only seemed to further inflame the uprising. They inquired about the object of Jona's message. Who was this Deliverer? They had heard rumors about his works and knew about what had transpired at the soup kitchen but that was all they knew. The head of the judicial courts, Judge Cappas, suggested to the Governor that perhaps "it would be better for one man to die than to bring war against all the people."

Governor Platt agreed that making a popular figure the scapegoat could quickly end the rioting, but he didn't think the charges could be proven in court. The Governor questioned if anyone had actually been harmed by this street walker. Chief Herold insisted that they had the power to make the law and enforce the law as they saw fit. Herold demanded that this man be dealt with ruthlessly. The Governor asked if Herold and his forces would be able to apprehend the man at the center of the uprising. Chief Herold answered affirmatively. They ended the meeting but were to gather later that evening to devise their plan.

After Jona's death, Emmanuel left the shelter taking no one with him. The residents who followed Emmanuel were in despair from the killing of their baptizer and now were adrift in the absence of their Teacher. Then, one day as they sat sullenly in the main room, the door opened and Emmanuel walked in from the street. They leapt up in joy at the sight of him. Following Emmanuel, another man walked in looking weary and confused.

"This is Thad. He is with us," Emmanuel said.

Immediately, Nathan came forward to welcome their new member and to show him around their home. He introduced him to the others who had come to believe in the words of Emmanuel.

That evening was spent together in quiet reflection. Emmanuel gathered with them for an hour and then left the room saying only that he needed to pray.

The next day, Emmanuel commenced the final phase leading to the fulfillment of his sacred mission.

Early in the morning, Nathan was going about his work when Emmanuel came up to him. He pulled Nathan by the arm and led him to an area outside of the main room. Then, he placed his arm on Nathan's shoulder and spoke to him. As Emmanuel spoke, Nathan became distraught and Emmanuel embraced his follower and believer. As Emmanuel continued speaking, Nathan dropped his head into his hands. His chest heaved and his knees trembled. Emmanuel held on to his friend. Emmanuel released him and spoke again. Nathan nodded. Emmanuel smiled and placed his hand on his forehead, bowed his head, and spoke as in prayer. Then, Emmanuel walked away as Nathan stood staring out the window.

In the afternoon Toma came to the shelter. He wanted to study for a test and found a table near the windows where he sat. A few minutes later, Emmanuel came to see him. He took a chair and sat directly across from Toma. Then, Emmanuel spoke to the young man. As he listened, Toma's face contorted in pain. He leaned back in his chair and cupped his hands over his mouth. Emmanuel continued speaking. Toma put both his hands over his face and dropped his head into his lap. Emmanuel put his arm on Toma's shoulder. Toma lifted his head and wiped his face. Emmanuel spoke to him and Toma nodded. Emmanuel smiled and placed his hand on Toma's forehead and spoke with his head bowed. Emmanuel walked away as Toma stared out the window.

Then, Petros arrived at the shelter with groceries. He brought Andy with him. Emmanuel came over to them and embraced Andy. He directed him to the kitchen to get something to eat and Andy cheerily complied. Emmanuel put his arm around Petros and led him to a quiet space. Emmanuel began to speak. Petros interrupted him several times in protest. Emmanuel continued speaking. Petros shook his head to the side as if to question what he was hearing. Petros interrupted again and spoke with his voice raised. Emmanuel spoke further, but Petros shook his head vigorously. Emmanuel took both of Petros hands into his own and kept speaking. Petros shook off the hold that Emmanuel had on him and exclaimed, "Never! Not three times, not twice, not once! I will never deny you, Lord!" They stood apart and then Emmanuel turned and left.

As evening fell upon the town, the residents prepared for bed. They cleaned up the area and then gathered together to pray as Emmanuel had taught them. As they went to their beds, Emmanuel came over to Jamie. He took Jamie by the arm and they walked to a quiet space. He put his arm on Jamie's shoulder and spoke to him. He spoke for a long time as Jamie listened observantly. Then they looked at each other in silence. Finally, Jamie said something to Emmanuel. They both turned their heads to look into the room where Jonny was sitting. Emmanuel spoke to Jamie and Jamie nodded while keeping his gaze fixed on his brother. Emmanuel put his hand on Jamie's forehead, bowed his head, and spoke. Then he took Jamie into his arms and held him.

The next morning, Jonny saw Emmanuel walk quietly out the door. He couldn't stop thinking about the private conversations Emmanuel had with the others and he wanted to find out what it was all about. He put Blue on the leash and walked after Emmanuel, staying well behind so as not to be discovered.

Emmanuel walked to the park along the river's edge. He took a winding trail through the leafy trees that lead up a steep hill. He scaled the hill and came upon a plateau that looked down over the river. Jonny climbed up the hill, as well. When Emmanuel had ascended to the top, Jonny took Blue and they hid behind a large bush. He turned to his companion and held his index finger to his lips to instruct the dog to be quiet.

Standing alone on the hill, Emmanuel cupped his hands together in front of him and bowed his head as if in prayer. He lifted his gaze skyward to face the brightly shining sun while broadly extending his arms with palms raised upward. Emmanuel called out:

"Father!"

The sound of his voice echoed across the earth. Then, dazzling rays of white light flashed down from the sky and drenched Emmanuel in adorning grace. A gust of wind whisked through the trees making a sound like that of a strummed mandolin. Emmanuel's body lifted off the earth. From high above the clouds, a deep and booming voice reverberated across the land below:

"My Son."

The hilltop sparkled with brilliant illumination as the wind sung its sweet song. Emmanuel stood above the world and was one with the light. His bodily figure was transfigured to heavenly radiance as the beams of light poured through him. Again, the voice resounded:

"My Son."

Jolted by the blinding light, Jonny fell awkwardly on his back. Dazed, he righted himself and rubbed his eyes. Just then, a hand pulled back the branches of the bush and a face peered through the opening.

"Why are you hiding?"

It took a moment for him to recognize that it was the face of Emmanuel appearing from the light.

Jonny stammered, "I...I was following you."

"I told you to follow me, remember? You are being a good student." said Emmanuel. He came around the bush and sat down in front of Jonny with his legs crossed.

Jonny was awestruck by what he had witnessed.

"Wh-what just happened?" he asked anxiously.

Emmanuel patted Blue on the head and then said to Jonny, "There are some things we should talk about."

"You mean like the way you have been talking to the others?"

"Yes," said Emmanuel. "Like that."

"Were you going to tell me if I hadn't seen what just happened?"

Emmanuel paused for a moment then said, "Some things can be hard to understand, especially for a young boy."

"But I'm the one who has to write about what happens to you. You told me that, too, remember?"

Emmanuel nodded his head and smiled, "Yes, I did." He looked at Jonny and said gently, "I will tell you."

Jonny reached into his back pocket for his journal, but Emmanuel placed his hand on Jonny's arm and said, "Listen to me. You'll remember what I say. And when you need to know more, there is a Voice of Truth I will send to you when I am gone."

"What do you mean, 'when you are gone'? Where are you going?"

"I have a sacred mission to serve and a commandment to keep," Emmanuel told Jonny. "And that is to do the will of the Father who sent me. And His will is simply this: that those who believe in me, believe in God, and they will not perish into the world but will have life everlasting."

"That sounds like what you told Rabbi Nicholas when you enrolled me in religion classes."

"Yes, you are right," replied Emmanuel. "And to fulfill that mission I must be given to the world. And then, I will be raised up to the Father."

"What do you mean 'given to the world'?"

Emmanuel put his hand to his chin and thought for a moment. He furrowed his hand through the grass beneath him. He pulled out a tiny seed. "If this seed is spread upon the ground but not buried well, the birds will come and eat it. Or, if this seed falls upon a rock, it will die since it will receive no water. Or, if this seed is entangled into the thorns of wild bushes, it will be choked and will not grow. But, if this seed is planted in good, fertile ground it will grow lush and fill the plains with fresh grass." Emmanuel hesitated and asked Jonny, "Do you understand?"

"I think you're saying that the seed can bring new life, but only if it planted in a good way. Otherwise it will die."

"So it is. You understand well," Emmanuel answered. He held up the seed between his fingers. "The seed is like the word as I am the word. Those that hear me and keep my word, do God's will and live eternally. Those who do not heed my word and fall away to worldly temptation are condemned to death."

Jonny nodded in understanding. Then, he was shaken by a painful thought. "But the seed goes away," he said apprehensively. "Is that what you meant when you said 'when I am gone'?"

"Yes."

Jonny's eyes filled with tears.

"Soon I will be leaving you," Emmanuel said, "And then soon again, I will rise to live with the Father."

Jonny started to speak, "Are you going to be…"

Emmanuel interrupted Jonny and said, "I lay down my life of my own accord. No one of this world can take it from me. I lay my life down so that I will take it up again in God's heavenly kingdom."

Jonny cupped both of his hands over his face and dropped his head into his lap. After a few moments, he wiped the tears from his eyes and looked up to Emmanuel and asked, "Will I ever see you again?"

"God has a place for you in his home. He has a place for all of you and for everyone who follows me. Would I have taken you down this path if that were not so?"

Jonny said, "No. I know it's safe to go where you go."

"And you will be sent a Helper when I am gone," Emmanuel said. "You won't see him and you won't know of his presence but he will be with you always. And whatever you ask in my name, will be yours."

Puzzled, the boy asked, "How will that work?"

"With God, all things are possible," said Emmanuel.

"Okay, Emmanuel," Jonny said. "I trust you."

Emmanuel smiled and placed his hand on Jonny's forehead. He lifted his head and said, "Father, this is Jonny. He is most beloved by me. Bless him with your grace. I know him as he knows me and through me he knows you. He knows the word and honors the word and lives the word. I pray for him and the others whom you have given me. They were born to the world, but they are not of the world for they have risen above sin and temptation. Bless them with the truth. Your word is truth. And the truth is that you love them as you love me. I pray, too, for those who will believe in me through their works. They will abide in me and I in them, as I abide in the Father."

Emmanuel put his hand under Jonny's chin, lifted his head, and stared into his teary eyes.

"Love one another," he commanded. "As I have loved you, love one another. Love knows no fear because love is from God and God is love."

Jonny wiped the tears from his eyes and smiled at Emmanuel. "I love you, Emmanuel."

Emmanuel stood up and extended his arm to Jonny's and lifted him from the ground. "I already knew that," he told him with a pleasant smile.

They started the walk back to the shelter with Blue wagging his tail as he followed along tethered to the leash in Jonny's hand.

"Can I ask you a question?" Jonny inquired on their journey home. "When you pray, have you ever asked God something he hasn't answered?"

Emmanuel walked in silence as he reflected upon the question. Then he spoke, "I receive my commandments from God the Father and I know his word is true and I know the works I do are to serve him. I know my mission and my mission is to do God's will." He paused before continuing, "I know the time is coming when I will at last glorify God and honor Him as only the Son can honor the Father. I know the time is coming and so I lift my eyes in prayer to my Father and ask:

"Is this the day?"

"When will you know the answer?"

Emmanuel didn't speak but placed his arm over Jonny's shoulder as they continued to walk. A little while later, Jonny asked another question, "When you were standing on top of the hill and the light came shining down through you, I heard a voice say, 'My Son'. Was that God telling you something?"

Emmanuel smiled at the boy, "That was God telling you something."

They walked peacefully back down the hill and along the river finding their way to the shelter as the sun slipped beneath the horizon.

The next day, people gathered in the main room and listened to the radio broadcast. Emmanuel stood alone gazing out the window. The news was filled with reports of chaotic violence. The police were arresting anyone they believed to be a threat. Nevertheless, they faced escalating resistance. Groups of young people marched through the towns and protested loudly in front of government offices.

The radio broadcaster told of an incident at Capitol City where a teenaged protester climbed to the roof of the ten-story building housing the State tax offices. He stood above the cheering crowd below and raised a sign that said, "The Deliverer Comes!" The police spotted him and raced up to the roof. They grabbed the youngster and callously threw him off the rooftop to his death in full view of the shocked crowd.

The radio played a tape announcement from Chief Herold that said curfews and transit restrictions were being invoked immediately and that anyone caught in violation of the police authority would be severely punished. He went on to say that the police were aggressively pursuing a man at the center of the insurrection and required anyone with knowledge of him and his location to come forward with that information. He concluded by stating that anyone found to be in conspiracy with the revolt against the government would be considered an enemy of the State and would be dealt with harshly.

When the radio message from Herold was over, Emmanuel turned to face his followers. He said, "The time of my fulfillment is at hand."

Emmanuel walked upstairs as Jonny followed. He entered his mother's room. She was lying in her bed staring blankly at the wall. Her face was gaunt and her skin was pale. Emmanuel came to her bedside and leaned over and kissed her on the cheek. She looked at him without comprehension. She tried to speak, but only a gurgling noise was voiced. Emmanuel stood by, holding her hand. He bowed, put his hand on her forehead, and prayed, "Father, this is my mother. She is most beloved by me. Take her into your eternal kingdom and show her the grace and love she has shown me. It was you who sent me and it was she that cared for me as only a mother can. Bless her and embrace her in eternity."

After the blessing, Emmanuel released her hand. He reached behind him and pulled Jonny close to the bed. He took his mother's hand and placed it into Jonny's hand. He said, "Woman, here is your son."

She turned her gaze away from Emmanuel and looked into Jonny's face. She touched the curls of Jonny's hair and put her hand on his cheek. She said:

"My son."

Jonny stayed with her until her eyes closed shut. He put her hands on her stomach and quietly turned to leave the room. He looked for Emmanuel, but he was gone. He walked out into the hallway and saw Martha shaking her head as she said. "I don't know what he thinks he is doing with that old man. That Mr. Simon is the meanest man I have ever seen." She walked back to her nursing station. Jonny peered into the room where Mr. Simon stayed, the room they had passed by several times before.

Emmanuel was standing at the window. He drew open the shades to let in the light. Mr. Simon yelled at Emmanuel to leave him alone and get out of the room. Then Emmanuel went over to raise the sheets off the old man's legs. His feet were discolored from infection. The rank odor pervaded the room. Mr. Simon continued to berate Emmanuel as Emmanuel walked over to the sink and poured soap and water into a basin. He took the basin and two cloth towels with him and went to the end of the bed. He dipped one cloth into the warm, soapy water and began to wash Mr. Simon's feet. Mr. Simon tried to pull back his legs and swatted his arms at Emmanuel, but he was too weak. Emmanuel cleansed one foot and then began to clean the other. Mr. Simon started shaking his head and cried out, "Why are you doing this? I don't need you!" After both feet were bathed, he took the other cloth and slowly dried away the soap. Mr. Simon laid his head back on the pillow and began to weep. Emmanuel finished caring for him and replaced the sheets delicately over his legs. He returned the basin to the sink. He came to the bedside to stand over Mr. Simon.

Emmanuel placed his hand on Mr. Simon's forehead. He spoke to the old man. Mr. Simon nodded his head in affirmation at the questions asked of him. At last, when the rite was finished, Mr. Simon sat up in his bed and embraced Emmanuel. The old man lay back into his bed, folded his hands in front of him, and began to pray the last words given him by his savior.

CHAPTER SIXTEEN

On the day they stormed the shelter, the sun was bright in the sky and the wind was brisk. On the Police Captain's signal, armed troops wearing gas masks and flak jackets surrounded the building to ensure all escape paths were covered. Snipers took their positions in the building across the street and targeted their rifles at the shelter. Police cars blocked all paths to the road to make sure no vehicles could enter nor exit. Assault vehicles formed a perimeter around the shelter with marksmen in each equipped with fully loaded automatic weapons. Two ambulances were on standby. After four minutes, the Captain saw that everyone and everything was in place.

He gave the order to invade.

The front door was battered open and in charged a half-dozen attack forces. Three more rushed through the back. Five paratroopers rappelled from the roof to the upper floor and kicked in the windows as they flew in with weapons cocked.

Martha was on duty at her usual post on the third floor when the raid commenced. In seconds she was surrounded by the attackers. She was commanded to lock her hands behind her head. As she sat in astonishment, the Captain made his way to the third floor with a group of officers scurrying behind him.

"He's not on the first floor and he's not on the second floor. He must be here!" He saw Martha at her desk and menacingly came towards her. "Where is he? Tell me now if you know what's good for you!"

Martha looked at the crazed officer and stated, "I don't know what you want up here. All we have here are sick and disabled people. No one is a threat to you in any way."

The Captain pounded his fist on her desktop. "Not these morons. Where is the heretic called Emmanuel?" he shouted.

"You're looking for Emmanuel? Why didn't you say so?" Martha said as she unlocked her hands. "Emmanuel's gone."

"What do you mean, he's gone?"

"I mean, he left."

"Left where? We have people at the bus stations, at the train station, and the airport. There has been no report of anyone fitting his description at any of those places."

"All I can tell you is that he left this morning and he is definitely not here. Now, if you are through with your inquisition, I'm going to get back to my job so I can help all these people you just scared the heck out of."

As she walked past the Captain, he grabbed her arm and said, "Lady, if you were smart, you'd be worried about what we could do to you. What happened to that wild huckster Jona could happen to you."

Martha pulled his hand off her arm and jabbed her finger into his chest, "Mister, I am smart and I know what's going happen to me because Emmanuel told me so. But, if you were smart—and that appears to be a big if— you'd be real worried about what will happen to you." She glared at him and moved on to care for her patients.

The Captain lifted a walkie-talkie to his ear. He barked, "Tell Chief Herold he's not here. We're pulling out."

On the highway, the Colt pickup truck sped along as it

traveled north. After leaving quietly in the morning, they were nearing their destination. In the back, Jamie and Jonny sat on each side of the flatbed watching the landscape as Olde Town got further and further away. Emmanuel leaned against the back of the cab and lifted his face to the sun. Nathan sat in the passenger's seat with his bent arm sitting on the open window with Blue tucked in next to him. He turned to the driver and exclaimed over the noise of the wind buffeting the cab, "Nice truck you have, Thad."

Finally, they approached the downtown section of Capital City. The truck slowed to a crawl as it fell in behind the usual heavy afternoon traffic. They passed the jail where Jona had been imprisoned and where he was killed. Across the street was the soup kitchen. A long line of destitute people stood hoping for a meal. One of the men standing in line saw the Colt cruising down the street. Stefan pointed to the truck and yelled, "It's him! He's come back for us. It's the one Jona sang about. It's the Deliverer!" He ran past the line and hurried inside. Shortly, Felipe came out to join Stefan. He waved excitedly at his friends in the truck. Felipe ran through the streets and hopped onto the back of the truck.

"Emmanuel, we've been waiting for you!" said Felipe as he embraced Emmanuel. He hugged Jamie and Jonny and shook hands with Nathan who extended his arm from outside the car window.

Stefan ran up and down the street shouting, "It's the Deliverer!" People gazed at the truck and its occupants. Some began waving and clapping. The crowd following the truck grew larger and people from inside the downtown buildings came out to see what was happening. Those on the higher floors opened their windows and leaned out to catch a glimpse of the man they had heard so much about.

A young musician leaving orchestra hall heard the commotion and saw the people following Emmanuel on the Colt. He unbuckled his case and took out his trumpet. He began to play the chorus to Jona's song, "The Deliverer Comes." He tracked the truck while trumpeting the song as the crowd followed Emmanuel through town. The crowd began chanting in unison to the siren call of the horn:

Singing love,
Bringing love,
He is love,
The Deliverer comes.

Several police officers on duty saw the forming wave of people and tried to push against the crowd but were unable to hold them back. The truck rolled through Capital City with throngs of jubilant people following and clapping and singing along. Emmanuel witnessed the people's worship of him. He raised himself up and stood before the crowd and extended his arms. The crowd erupted in celebration.

Eventually, the truck passed by a trendy restaurant and a waiter there caught sight of Emmanuel standing above the crowd. He hurried to the kitchen grabbing a gourmet dish made with hearts of palm and rushed out to the truck bowing as he laid the offering at the feet of his redeemer. On and on, Emmanuel paraded through town as the people gave him their acclamation and praise.

The truck cleared the busy downtown area as the sounds of the adoring crowd faded away in the distance. They made their way to Felipe's home on the lake. Thad parked his truck in the driveway and they entered the house.

They took some time to rest and clean up from their journey. Then they all gathered on the back porch facing the lake where Felipe's boat was tied to the pier. A short time later, they heard a knock at the front door. Petros, Andy, and Toma had arrived from Olde Town and had come to Felipe's house. They embraced in fellowship. Nathan asked how they had traveled to Capital City. Toma explained that they took the early train but almost didn't make it.

"There were police officers everywhere doing security checks. When we were ready to board, they came up to us and asked us if we were from the shelter. We said we weren't, which is true, and then they asked us if we knew Emmanuel. Before I could answer, Petros told them that we didn't know Emmanuel. Then, he asked Andy the same question and Andy just grit his teeth and refused to answer and then Petros said none of us knew Emmanuel. And then a heavy-set officer with a thick mustache saw us and said we looked familiar to him. He asked us again if we knew Emmanuel, and Petros said no for the third time and grabbed Andy and me by the arm and got us on the train just as the doors were closing."

Petros looked at Emmanuel and lowered his head. Emmanuel came over, put his arm on Petros' shoulder and said, "Petros, I'm glad you are here with me," he said.

Felipe brought lemonade. They poured themselves a drink and began to talk enthusiastically of their trip. They exchanged stories, sometimes talking over each other in their excitement.

Nathan told them about when he was saved by Emmanuel from a drunken bully. Petros spoke of meeting Emmanuel when Officer Noble won the lottery ticket.

"I wrote a song for Emmanuel."

Toma told the story about Emmanuel saving Blue from drowning on the melted ice.

"I wrote a song for Emmanuel."

Felipe recalled Emmanuel feeding of the hungry at the soup kitchen. And even more stories than this were told but then Jamie spoke:

"Jonny has something he wants to say." Everyone stopped talking at the sound of Jamie's voice. When they were quieted, Jamie turned to his brother and tipped his head.

"I wrote a song for Emmanuel," said Jonny.

Nathan asked, "When did you do that?"

"When Jamie and me were traveling with Jona. I was reading the Scriptures and started to read the psalms. Jona told me that psalms during the time of Scripture are like songs of today. So he said we should write a song from one of the psalms." replied Jonny.

Someone asked, "Why do you need to turn the psalms into songs? Aren't they fine as they are?"

"Well, Jona talked about the Book of Isaiah and said it is good to speak to people in the ways they know best so that they…"

"So that they perceive what they see and understand what they hear and turn and be healed," interjected Emmanuel quoting the verse from Scripture. He smiled at Jonny. "Sing your song, Jonny."

Jonny took out his journal from his pocket. He paged to the song. "Jona said there was a certain psalm he thought about often. He said it made him think of the coming of the Messiah and the sacrifice he must endure. This song is from Psalm 22."

"My God, My God, why have you forsaken me," said Emmanuel.

Jonny nodded his head. He took a deep breath and closed his eyes. He thought of Jona playing the melody on his guitar. In a strong and steady voice, Jonny sang:

My God, have you forsaken me?
Have you forsaken me?
The morning's gone and so I plead,
Is this the day I'm freed?

Around me all these people,
Can you see their shame?
All around me is evil,
All around me is pain.

Glory, now I see the sun go down
The world has lost its hold on me.
Still I own the knowledge
Of life within me yet.

My God, you are who sent me here,
You have sent me here.
Their hardened hearts hinder them,
Listen and let me in.

The echoes fading slowly
As sky and sea come about.
Nobody's here to welcome me,
Nobody's here to shout.

Glory, now I see the sun go down
The world has lost its hold on me.
Take this life in ransom, Lord
Let your Kingdom come.

My God, you are to whom I pray,
The one to whom I pray.
In faith and trust I testify,
Make this the day I rise.

Lead them with your guiding light,
Keep them close in sight.
Deliver them from darkness, Lord
Join them with the Word.

Glory, now the sun has fallen down
My work is done and I am free.
The day is come and God I see,
I see, I Am!

Jonny ended his song. His friends looked at him in

amazement. Then, they applauded jubilantly. Emmanuel came out of his chair and lifted Jonny up into his arms and kissed him on the cheek.

A few minutes later, there was another knock on the front door. In walked Matilda with Magdalena, who was holding Lazarus in her arms. All the men warmly received the women and the baby. They invited them to join them on the porch. Lemonade was poured for them and Felipe went to prepare milk for Lazarus.

Magdalena said that her sister had told her of Emmanuel's trip to Capital City. Rabbi Nicholas also knew of the trip and they drove together taking along Matilda, as well. The men cheerfully told Matilda of the song Jonny sang to them based on her class assignment. She told them how impressed she has been with Jonny's writing in school.

They sat together on the porch as the sunlight over the lake began to dim. After some further conversation they all grew quiet. Emmanuel regarded those gathered around him. He told them, "I'm glad you are all here with me."

"I'm glad we're here, too," exclaimed Andy. Then he wrinkled his face and innocently added, "Christos, why are we here?"

Petros winced at the child's awkward question, but Emmanuel just laughed pleasantly. He leaned forward, brought his hands to his chin, and paused in silence as the others focused their attention on him. Then he said:

"Soon I will be leaving you," he told his friends.

"I want to go with you!" Andy called out boisterously. Petros put his arm around his son in comfort.

Emmanuel said plainly, "I am going where you can't follow." He assessed all who were assembled before him. "But be happy for me because the Father beckons. I was with him before the world was, and the hour of my homecoming approaches."

Magdalena started to weep as she rocked Lazarus in her arms.

"Your sorrow will pass and turn into joy. I go to the Father and, soon again, I will come to you and raise you up to my Father's house."

Then Felipe made a request, "Emmanuel, show us the Father so we will know where the path leads."

Emmanuel hung his head, shook it slightly, and said in exasperation, "Do you not yet know the truth? Have you not witnessed the works I have done? Don't you see the path I have revealed?"

Toma interjected, "Teacher, show us the way."

Emmanuel pounded his fist on the table, "I am the way!" he thundered.

They stared at Emmanuel in stunned silence. He looked at each of them with his eyes gleaming. His face softened, he breathed deeply, and he extended his arms in embrace of them all.

"I am the way and I am the truth and I am life."

He reached out his hands to them. They clasped their hands in his and in each other's.

"Believe in me and believe in God who sent me. You are the light to the world. Let your light shine upon all so that they will know God as you know me."

They nodded in understanding. Emmanuel released his grip on them.

"The time is coming when the ruler of this world will assert his dominion, but his rule will be vanquished. I will reveal God's heavenly kingdom when I am resurrected. When I am risen, the truth of eternal life will be known. Hear my words and believe."

"Amen," they answered in unison.

"The hour draws near, then," Emmanuel responded. "You will be separated and I must go alone. Do not fear for me. God is with me. Be at peace. I am born to conquer the world. I am born for this moment."

They sat together in quiet reflection. Then, Felipe said supper was ready. They went inside and each helped in preparing the table. Jonny tied Blue to the back post and left him with fish trimmings and fresh water. Felipe brought out the food while Thad uncorked the wine. Petros sliced the fish that Felipe had prepared as Andy discarded the bones. Toma carefully removed the bread that had been cooking in the oven. Nathan and Jamie put out chairs for everyone, putting Emmanuel's place at the head. Matilda set the plates.

"Besides Emmanuel, is that ten place settings we need?" asked Matilda. At the same time, Lazarus started to whimper.

"Make that eleven, my baby is hungry, too," Magdalena said as they laughed in harmony.

Just then, they heard a sharp knock at the front door to Felipe's house.

"Sounds like twelve!" Matilda said as they continued to chuckle.

Felipe went to the door and re-entered the dining room looking grim.

"It's the reporter. She heard you were on your way to Capital City and she went to the soup kitchen. When she saw I wasn't there, she asked one of our volunteers where I lived. She wants to see you."

Emmanuel reluctantly got up from the table and made his way to the front door. Before he got there, Judith barged into the room. She saw Emmanuel coming towards her and grinned broadly.

"I'm so glad you're here." She looked around the room. "Oh, so many of your friends are here for dinner. Do you have room for one more?" No one answered. "I see," she replied flatly. She faced Emmanuel, lowered her voice, and asked, "Well, can I speak with you? There are so many things our audience wants to know about you." As she spoke, she deftly reached into her purse.

Emmanuel told her, "This is not your place."

"Of course it's my place. You're the greatest story of our time and I'm the one and only person who has ever interviewed you. Our broadcasts about you have never had higher ratings. Everyone wants to know about you. They want to know if you're the Deliverer that your friend Jona told them about." She looked at Emmanuel and said, "Jona died for you. He died so you would be known. You owe him this."

"You are right. Jona spoke of my coming. He also said, 'those born of earth know earthly things, but the one sent from above is above all'. I owe God who sent me. And that debt is about to be paid," Emmanuel told her.

"What about those in government who take care of all these needy people? Don't you owe them allegiance?" she asked.

"I speak openly of whom I honor."

"In the State, the highest honor is to the Governor. Do you accept his authority?"

"Authority comes from God and his word."

"How do you know the word of God?"

"I am the word of God."

"So you claim sovereignty over the people, then."

"You say it is so."

"And you reject the authority of the Governor?"

"You can't serve two masters. I serve God alone."

"So you admit to rejecting the authority of the Governor and the laws of the State?"

"I was born into the world to speak the truth."

"What is the truth?"

"Whoever believes in me shall live, and whoever does not, will die."

"What you're saying is you condemn people to death if you judge that they don't observe your beliefs."

"Their sins condemn themselves," Emmanuel said. "I am not sent to judge the world. I am sent to save the world." Then, he took her hand in his and said to her, "It's not too late for you to be saved. Your road leads to perdition, but you can still take the narrow and righteous path. You have a choice."

"You would save me?" she asked. "What if I betrayed

you to the authorities? Would you save me even then?"

"I pray for those who persecute me. I pray for you. I pray for your salvation, and salvation can be yours, if only you believe."

"But I have so much here to lose."

"You have everything to gain."

Her eyes grew moist as she listened to the man who was offering her eternity.

Judith stood in silence considering her fate. Finally, she leaned into him, kissed him on the cheek and said, "I'm sorry," and left.

The others had stopped their preparations for supper but quietly, now, they resumed.

When supper was ready, they gathered together for the last time and took their places at the table. Emmanuel looked around the table. He smiled affectionately.

"Thank you."

His friends surveyed each other. "You are Emmanuel the Christ. You have given to us in great abundance yet we have done nothing for you," one said.

"You are with me. You have listened to my teachings and taken my words for your own. You love one another as I love you. I have been sent into the world to serve God's commandment and now that work will be finished and it falls to you to bear the burden of the world. And it will be a heavy burden and the road will be filled with hatred and persecution. So, I ask the Father to sanctify you with the truth. Your witness will bear much fruit. Like the vine, you are the branches, and the fruit you bear will glorify God. You are my disciples. You will bring my words to people everywhere and they will become disciples, too. And one day, we will all be joined in God's eternal kingdom."

Petros, who was seated next to Emmanuel, lowered his gaze. "Emmanuel, I am weak next to you and my sins are many" he confessed. "How can we carry on your glory?"

"Can you tend for those who are in need?

"Yes, I can."

"Will you speak the truth of my word to those who seek God?"

"Yes, Christos, I will."

"Do you love me as I love you?"

"You know I do."

Emmanuel laid his hand on Petros' shoulder saying, "You are the rock upon which my church will be built."

Petros lowered his head saying, "I will follow you to my death."

"And then you will live forever with me in God's house where there are many mansions and where a place has been set for all of you and for all whom you commend to God," Emmanuel promised.

Then Emmanuel took the basket in front of him. He broke off a wedge of bread and passed the basket around the table.

"I came to you in body and in blood. In remembrance of me, take this bread as a symbol of my body which I give up for you."

They each ate of the bread. Then he took the bottle of wine. He poured a cup and then passed it around the table.

"Take this wine as a symbol of the blood I shed for you."

They each drank of the wine.

"This covenant is the sign of my fidelity in you. I will abide in you as you abide in me."

They completed the ritual signifying Emmanuel's living presence in them. They continued with the meal as they expressed their fellowship and confirmed their devotion to Emmanuel. After their meal was consumed, they cleared the table and sat together in the living room. Thad, the newest disciple, raised a question: "Emmanuel, what is most important for us to know?"

"Your duty is to love God with all your heart, all your mind, and all your strength. There is nothing greater than this. And you are called to love your neighbor as I have loved you. No one can love more than to lay down his life for a friend. And I call you friends. As my friends, I have made everything known to you. I depart the world, now go to the world and bear witness to God's love. You are chosen for this purpose and it is for this purpose you are ordained. These are my commandments. Honor them and God will be with you as I am with you."

"But when we go out into the world in your name, how will people know we have been chosen by you?" asked Felipe.

Emmanuel answered, "They will know you are mine by your love." He looked at each of them and said, "Live as I have lived, love as I have loved, and I will be manifest in you."

"How will you be manifest in us if you are gone from the world?" wondered Thad.

"I am sent by the Father to walk the streets of the world and to be his word made flesh. When I am gone, God will send another in my name; not in body, but in Spirit. The Holy Spirit will be your help and will remind you of everything I have said and all that I have done. The truth will be in you as I am in you. You see, it will be to your advantage for the Holy Spirit to come in my place," Emmanuel assured them. "All that you seek in my name, will be given you. When you are tired, the Holy Spirit will be your Comforter; when you are in need the Holy Spirit will be your Advocate; when you have questions, the Holy Spirit will be your Counselor. Ask, and you will receive."

"When will the Holy Spirit come to us?" one disciple asked voicing the question they all had.

"The Holy Spirit will come to you when I am gone. The Spirit is in me as I am with the Father. You will not be alone for the Holy Spirit's baptism comes soon. I tell you this now so you will believe when the Holy Spirit comes upon you.

"And when the Holy Spirit comes, he will admonish those who preached against sin but didn't heed their own counsel. In death, people will see their sins revealed and upon my rising, God's righteousness will be confirmed. Denunciation will be the fate of the kings and monarchs who failed to follow the light.

"I have more to say but it is more than you can bear now. But when the Holy Spirit comes, he will guide you to the truth. The Voice of Truth will come to you when you ask and when you ask, the words will come. Let the words of truth flow through you like living water."

Suddenly, Blue began to bark and growl. The house hushed in apprehension.

"Do not despair," Emmanuel said. "The ruler of this world comes. The time of my fulfillment arrives."

Just then both the front and back doors were kicked in and a swarm of armed soldiers invaded the home. Blue kept barking and Lazarus cried loudly. A soldier barked out, "Where is he?" He looked about the room and saw the man seated at the head of the table. He came closer, "Are you the one they call Emmanuel?"

Emmanuel stood up and said, "I am."

The soldier paused confused by the swift declaration. He pulled out handcuffs to place them on Emmanuel. Petros jumped up and forcefully hurled the soldier to the ground. Another soldier immediately drew out his gun and aimed it at Petros.

"Papa!" cried Andy.

Emmanuel appeared between the attacker and Petros. The soldier pulled the trigger.

The gun misfired.

Incredulous, the soldier looked at the gun. He cocked the weapon and again pointed it at his target. Emmanuel put one hand on the weapon and the other on the soldier's arm and calmly lowered them.

"Do what you came to do. I will not harm you." Then Emmanuel turned his head, looked to his disciples, and said, "I leave you in peace, my peace I give you."

The first soldier lifted himself off the ground and put

handcuffs on Emmanuel. He steered him out of the home with his colleagues ensuring that none of the others followed.

Outside, flashing lights from police cars and assault vehicles illuminated the dark night.

Directly in front of the home was a single floodlight atop of a video camera pointed at the red-headed woman speaking into a microphone.

"This is your investigative reporter, Judith, with an exclusive report from the far south side. Behind me is the home of an accomplice of Emmanuel. Based on a confidential tip, the police together with the State military have executed a raid at this location. Tonight, I am the first to announce to our audience this breaking news: Emmanuel, the one some call the Christ, has been taken captive and is under arrest. He is being brought to the penitentiary under heavy guard. I am told by my sources that he will be charged with multiple offenses the most serious of which is treason against the State.

"Sources say that the prosecutors have been ordered by senior government officials to seek the fullest measure of punishment under the law: death by hanging."

CHAPTER SEVENTEEN

In the ensuing days, the rioting that had persisted across the State diminished. People were fixated on the coming trial of the State v. Emmanuel.

In the Statehouse, high level meetings were held day and night to develop the evidence and to prepare their case. Governor Platt met with Judge Cappas and Chief Herold many times. The lead prosecutor assigned, Mr. Amos, was involved in those meetings. They agreed to the charges being brought, but they differed as to the punishment. The Governor did not think the death penalty was warranted. Chief Herold was adamant that Emmanuel should be put to death to ensure that no other fraudulent brokers of salvation would follow in his place.

Finally, the day came when the trial was to commence. The Chief assigned extra security to safeguard the entire building. Reporters jammed the court room. Some citizens were allowed in to view the proceedings from the gallery. Nathan assumed the role of Emmanuel's lawyer, although no one had any contact with Emmanuel since his arrest. Jonny and Jamie were allowed to sit behind Nathan. The morning session was taken for jury selection. Twelve men and women from Capital City were chosen as jurors. In the afternoon, the trial began.

The lead prosecutor and his staff entered the court room. As Mr. Amos put his papers across the desk, a fellow prosecutor came up and handed him a thick file folder. From the other table, Jonny could see the words, 'Prosecution case against Stefan' typed on the folder. The two colleagues had an animated conversation and then the unidentified prosecutor put his card on top of the file and briskly left the court room. As he left, his card blew off the table and landed near Jonny's foot. He called to the man who had dropped it, but he didn't hear. Jonny picked up the card which read, "Paolo di Taurasi, State Prosecutor" and placed it in his pocket.

A door opened and in walked Emmanuel with two guards at his side. His beard had grown thicker and his hair had grown long and wavy. He was thinner and there were noticeable bruises on his face. He saw Nathan and nodded to him. Then he saw Jonny and Jamie and smiled. The jury was seated and Judge Cappas entered the room and was seated at the bench. He gaveled the trial to order.

Mr. Amos gave the opening statement. He made the case against Emmanuel. He reviewed the evidence and witnesses that would be presented to prove that Emmanuel was not just a fraud, but an enemy of the State.

The Judge asked Nathan for his opening statement. Nathan looked at Emmanuel who merely shook his head. Nathan told the Judge they would not offer a statement. Judge Cappas asked the prosecution to call its witnesses. The prosecutor called Stefan to the stand.

The police had received a tip that Stefan had gotten the secret tape made by Jona and mailed it to the shelter in Olde Town. Based on that, they indicted Stefan on charges of illicit transport of contraband and conspiring to aid the seditious activities of Jona. Stefan was arrested soon after Emmanuel and was to be put on trial separately. The State wanted Stefan as a witness first and, after he had been examined, he would be returned to jail pending his own trial. Amos opened the large file folder he had just received from his associate.

"When did you first meet the defendant, Emmanuel?" Amos asked as he began the interrogation.

"I met him that day when he came to the soup kitchen and fed hundreds of starving people," answered Stefan.

"You say he fed hundreds of people. How?"

"I don't know how. It was a miracle. I've been at the soup kitchen for months and nothing like that had ever happened before."

"Did the food just magically appear?"

"Food appeared, yes."

"Are you sure he didn't steal it from somewhere?"

"No, I'm sure he didn't steal it. This is a great man, a kind man."

"Then tell me, if this man, a great man, so you say, can make food magically appear, why didn't he do it again?"

Stefan paused momentarily and then shrugged his shoulders. "I don't know," he said.

"What I'm trying to find out is if it is so easy for this man to make food appear why doesn't he just do it all the time, for everyone who is hungry? Wouldn't that be the act of a kind man?" Stefan didn't have an answer so the prosecutor continued. "No, instead of doing his magic again, he leaves it to the State to feed the hungry. And the State is dutiful in supplying poor people with their needs." Amos raised his voice and went on, "But this man presumes through some deception or some thievery to be a servant to the people and then never returns to them; he just leaves them hungry. And in leaving them hungry incites their rebellion against the State because this fraud leads the people to believe the State has failed them. Isn't that right?"

Stefan shook his head, "No, that's not right!"

"Then where am I wrong?" asked Amos.

"You're wrong in calling him a fraud. He's not a fraud, he is the truth."

"The truth?"

"The truth that anyone who tastes of the bread that Emmanuel provides will have salvation. When you know that truth, one sacramental meal is all you need. Everyone who accepted the food Emmanuel offered that day was witness to the truth. His is the food sent from heaven to grant life everlasting. When you share of that food and consume that blessing, your salvation is assured."

Amos stumbled over his follow-up question and, after paging through the file folder, moved to another subject.

"You are under arrest for aiding in the sedition of Jona, isn't that correct?"

"That is what you have arrested me for," responded Stefan.

"Did you not transport material from an imprisoned man and covertly send it to the defendant?"

"I took a gift from a righteous man named Jona and sent it as he requested to a holy man named Emmanuel. I make no apologies for that, sir."

"You don't see the incendiary impact of that song you transported in fostering riots in the streets?" barked the prosecutor.

"All I see is the State condemning the righteous and the holy." Stefan exclaimed.

"Objection, Your Honor!" interrupted Amos.

Cappas banged his gavel and instructed Stefan to keep his responses to the questions posed.

Amos went into another line of questioning, "Your disrespect is the very example of what this man has provoked in the citizenry and the reason he must be stopped. But let me ask you one last question before you are returned to your jail cell. You speak so dismissively about the State and the government. Isn't that a tactic to promote the anarchist agenda of people like Jona and Emmanuel who encourage your dangerous rants? You undermine the law by breaking the law. You seek to conquer government by ridiculing government. Isn't that the aim of your sedition and treason?"

"I don't take aim at the government, the government takes aim at me," Stefan declared. "I am a man brought to life by God's design and I am endowed with the freedom he bestows. I choose to be a servant of God. I choose to be a disciple to the teaching of the man who sits before me, the man in whose eyes I see heaven; the man you seek to defile. He is not an enemy of the King of this nation or of the Governor of this State or of anyone in this world."

Stefan scanned the room and saw people listening in rapt attention. He continued saying, "From the beginning it has been so that authorities garner their power by usurping the freedoms of the people. When the tribes of Israel were under the oppression of Egypt, Moses led his people through the wilderness to flee from their tyrants. Over generations, governmental authorities have limited the rights of the people while corruptly expanding their own power. The Romans, in their empire, created a class system of free and slave reserving privilege to the ruling few. Who were they to indenture those whom God has made?

"The Ottomans, in their era, gave powers to the Sultan that subjugated the faiths of the religious to the dictates of the State. The Chinese in the Ming dynasty established a bureaucracy dedicated to spying on its own people, and then would ruthlessly deploy its military at the merest hint of rebellion, even as millions starved under their reign. Does this sound familiar? And what of the Russians who in recent generations rampaged across Europe in mass conquest to sustain its crumbling economy by preying upon weaker nations.

"Was benevolence the aspiration of the Egyptians, the Romans, the Turks, the Chinese, or of the Russians in forging their dominions? Or, was it, rather, the lust for supremacy by the elite and the powerful? Who made them ruler and judge over us?

"Imagine people free," Stefan continued. "People free

to express their faith in God, free to exercise their skills, free to raise a family. Imagine how wonderful it would be. How much more would we achieve if our lives were fueled by God's grace and we had the freedom and the faith to embrace it. You see, God is the God of all, of all nations and of all people.

"Consider this country in which we live, America, a nation of separate states. You say we owe allegiance to this State because it provides for the people. But it is not allegiance you seek, it is compulsion. And therein is the tyranny of an oppressive government: it takes hostage the free will of the people.

"You ask who is to provide for the people, if not the State? I say, it is not for the State, it is for the people to provide. And they will provide, for themselves and for others, when they exercise the freedom God has conferred upon them. Our allegiance is owed only to God who gives us life, and it is in God that we prosper.

"I am not against the government," Stefan stated. "I am for God."

Stefan softened his voice and told a story: "When I was a young boy, I heard about a special comet that was dashing through the earth's atmosphere. We were told by the astronomers that we would be able to see the comet in the night sky with the naked eye. It had been discovered by a British scientist named Halley one hundred and eighty-one years before that transcendent time of my youth. I stayed up all night waiting and searching.

"Then it flashed across the sky, leaving a trail of sparkling light as it darted through the blackness. In that moment, I came to believe in the hope of a new life born from the light. The astronomers say that this comet, which had come to me as a boy, is once again on a trajectory to return to the earth's sky when I will be very old, if I get to be very old. I pray that when it does, it will pass by a world that knows the light and lives in the light, though I fear that the world will still yet endure in darkness. This man, the one you claim is a traitor, is the light. Through him we have hope, in him we know love, and with him we will find God.

"And so this is the sum and substance of my testimony: Follow him."

Stefan looked at the men and women of the jury. He raised his arm and directed their attention to Emmanuel.

"This man speaks the truth, and the truth will free us," he professed. "He is not an enemy of the State, nor is he any enemy to any people. This man is our greatest blessing, the hope of the world, our prince of peace. He is our light and our salvation. He is our Savior. This man is Emmanuel the Christ."

There was silence as the impact of his words hung in the room. After a long pause, the prosecutor stood up.

"Your Honor, I move that this witness' testimony be stricken from the record. He was unresponsive to the question and simply made a long speech rather than testify to the facts of this case."

Judge Cappas mumbled and finally said, "Hmm, yes, I see that, of course that's right."

Amos replied, "I move that his entire testimony be stricken, except for his confession that he transported illicit materials from Jona to Emmanuel, which will be included in his upcoming felony trial."

"So ordered," commanded Cappas. "Jury, you are instructed to disregard all the testimony you have just heard. In no way should this be part of your judgment in this trial for treason."

Stefan stood from his chair and pointed to the Judge, "You commit treason on our trust! You violate the law you vow to uphold with your deception, but I will not yield to your exploitation. I stand before the Son of God, and I will not be moved. My testimony is true and my faith is entrusted to Emmanuel!"

The Judge directed the guards to forcibly remove Stefan from the court room. Two brawny officers hoisted him by his arms and carried him out of the chair. He struggled and they threw him to the ground. His head bounced off the edge of the defendant's table and he collapsed to the floor. Blood trickled down his cheek from above his eye. He looked up and saw Emmanuel gazing at him. "Messiah, forgive them. They know not their sins."

Emmanuel looked upon Stefan and said, "The day comes when you will be with me in heaven." The guards dragged Stefan away leaving a bloody trail on the stone floor.

Cappas gaveled the court to order. He repeated his instruction to the jury to disregard Stefan's testimony. He admonished the people in the gallery to maintain order or they would be held in contempt of court. He turned to the prosecutor and told him to call the next witness.

Judith was called to the stand.

The prosecutor asked her about how she first met Emmanuel and she went on to describe the day at the soup kitchen when hundreds had been miraculously fed. She talked about the interview she conducted with Emmanuel. He asked her if there was anything in particular that struck her about the interview.

"He said he was who God sent."

"He was who God sent?"

"That's what he said."

Then the prosecutor asked what happened after the interview.

"Nothing," she replied. "He just went away and wasn't heard from. I kept on getting questions about doing a follow-up story. My editor," she said as she tipped her head to the direction of her editor sitting in the gallery, "said he wanted another exclusive interview. But we just didn't know where he was. He could have contacted me, or anyone, any time and we would have put him on the air. It was like he didn't want to be known."

"So how did you eventually find him?"

"One day, I read a story about a little girl at Olde Town

Community Hospital who was dying of sickle cell anemia and then received a blood transfusion that cured her. And then, just a short time later, I heard a about another girl in Olde Town who had been crippled by polio but who can now walk. And then there was a news report from our radio station in Olde Town about a deaf boy who saved his school from a potential gas explosion and then suddenly learned how to speak. With all these incredible things happening, I decided that I should go to Olde Town to see what was happening there."

"When you went there, what did you find out?"

"I found out he was living at the homeless shelter."

"He was living at the homeless shelter in a poor downstate town?" the prosecutor inquired with disdain. "This man who described himself as 'who God sent' living in a homeless shelter?"

"Yes."

"So then you went to this homeless shelter to find him. And did you find him there?"

"I did, but he wouldn't speak to me."

"Why wouldn't he speak to you? After all, you're a popular news reporter who wanted to tell people about what he was doing to help them, isn't that so?"

"That's what I told him. But he wouldn't speak to me."

"So you left?"

"Well, I managed to spend some time talking with the residents there," she replied and looked briefly at Jonny.

"I see. Can you recall what you learned?"

Nathan raised an objection on the basis that this was hearsay and not direct testimony of the facts. Amos said he would be happy to call the residents to the stand and interrogate each of them. Emmanuel just shook his head. Nathan withdrew the objection.

Amos continued his questioning, "Please go ahead and tell us what you heard."

"I heard truly amazing stories. I heard about the young girl with the blood disease he cured, I heard about a crippled girl who now walks, I heard about…"

Prosecutor Amos interrupted and said, "In the interest of time, let me ask you about a couple specific stories. Were you told about a lottery ticket and a police officer?"

"Yes. The story was that a police officer was shopping at a store when Emmanuel gave him a lottery ticket."

"Emmanuel gave him a lottery ticket?"

"Yes, and it turned out that this was the winning lottery ticket. From those winnings, the police officer got an operation for his…"

"Yes, we know that the police officer used the winnings from the lottery to get an operation for his son. What I want to verify is that it was the defendant who had the lottery ticket in his possession and gave it to the officer?"

"That's what I was told."

"Your Honor," said Amos as he turned his attention to the judge, "as you know there was a claim of malfeasance involving that lottery which the State has been rigorously investigating. We interviewed the police officer in question and he has given us a sworn statement saying that the winning lottery ticket was given to him by Emmanuel." Amos handed the statement to the judge. "We don't know the mechanism by which the defendant knew in advance the number that was drawn but we believe strongly this is an act of counterfeiting and fraud. Consequently, we move to add the charge of conspiracy to commit fraud as part of the State's prosecution."

"So ordered."

Contented, Amos resumed his interrogation. "Let me ask about one other incident. Were you told about a woman and a newborn baby?"

"Yes, I was."

"Please tell the court what you were told."

"One day, Emmanuel hurried away from the shelter and rushed to the clinic looking for a certain woman," Judith said.

"He was looking for a woman?"

"Yes. Apparently she worked there."

"How well did he know this woman?"

"He knew her well enough to charge into the clinic, storm past the other employees, and march into a restricted surgical area."

"Then what happened?" asked Amos.

"After a while, Emmanuel, and this woman came out with a baby. And then, the two of them together, just left the clinic and took the baby with them."

"Let me repeat this for the jury: the defendant broke into a restricted area of the clinic, found a woman that he had some relationship with, and then they both took off with a newborn baby. Is that your testimony?"

Judith slowly reached into her purse for a handkerchief, theatrically dabbed her eyes, and said, "Yes."

The prosecutor went to his desk, picked up a sheet of paper and brought it to the Judge. "Your Honor, this is a statement attested to by the woman named Magdalena corroborating the account of this witness. We move to incorporate a charge of kidnapping as part of the State's prosecution. A similar charge will be made against the woman pending her continued cooperation in this matter."

The Judge read the paper. He decreed, "So ordered."

Nathan jumped out of his chair, "That's not what happened! The baby was dead and Emmanuel brought it back to life. He saved the child. He didn't kidnap him."

The Judge barked at Nathan, "That will be for the jury to decide. Now sit down."

Cappas turned to Amos and said, "Continue."

The prosecutor pranced in front of the jury examining the expression on their faces. He turned to face Judith. "I just have one more line of questioning. Did you have any other meetings with the defendant?"

"Yes," Judith answered, "on the night he was arrested, I discovered the home on the south side where he and his friends were having supper."

"You went there and were you able to speak to him?"

"Yes."

"Do you remember what he told you the night he was arrested for treason against the State?"

"I don't need to remember it," she said. "I taped it."

"Do you have the tape with you?"

"I do."

"Now, you do understand that as a member of the press, you can assert protection against the naming of sources as well as make claims of privileged use of taped information you've garnered."

"I do understand that."

"And?"

Judith looked at her editor in the gallery and then turned her head to look at Emmanuel. "I've made a choice." She reached into her purse and pulled out a tape. She handed it to Amos who loaded it into a tape player. He fast forwarded the tape to a predefined location.

"Your Honor, with the permission of the court, I would like to play the taped discussion between the witness and the defendant."

Nathan stood up. "We have no way of knowing how this tape has been handled or edited, Your Honor."

"If your client disputes that the tape is him speaking, you can object to it being submitted into evidence." Cappas responded sharply and nodded to Amos who pressed the play button. A segment of the conversation between Judith and Emmanuel at the last supper before Emmanuel's arrest was replayed. It began with Judith's voice:

"What about those in government who take care of all these needy people? Don't you owe them allegiance?"

"I speak openly of whom I honor."

"In the State, the highest honor is to the Governor. Do

you accept his authority?"

"Authority comes from God and his word."

"How do you know the word of God?"

"I am the word of God."

"So you claim sovereignty over the people, then."

"You say it is so."

"And you reject the authority of the Governor?"

"You can't serve two masters. I serve God alone."

"So you admit to rejecting the authority of the Governor and the laws of the State?"

"I was born into the world to speak the truth."

"What is the truth?"

"Whoever believes in me shall live, and whoever does not, will die."

"What you're saying is you condemn people to death if you judge that they don't observe your beliefs."

"Their sins condemn themselves…"

The prosecutor abruptly pressed the stop button on the tape recorder cutting off Emmanuel's voice mid-sentence. He walked to the jury box. While looking at the jurors, he addressed Judith, "You asked the defendant if he rejected the authority of the Governor and he said that is so. Does that tape reflect what he said to you, what came out of his own mouth?"

"Yes, it does. All of it does."

"Even the part where he said that the people condemn themselves to death?"

"Yes, all of it," Judith concluded.

Amos shook his head in disbelief as he faced the jurors. Then he turned to speak to the judge. "Judge Cappas said he would give the defense a chance to object if it really wasn't the defendant speaking those words. Is there an objection?"

Nathan sat motionless in his chair.

"I didn't think so," Amos said derisively. He walked back to his desk, shuffled through some papers, and without looking at her said, "The witness is dismissed."

Judith remained fixed in her seat unsure as to what would happen next. The Judge echoed Amos, "You are dismissed. We don't need you anymore."

Slowly, she got up from her seat and walked to the court room door. She paused as she passed Emmanuel but didn't face him. She stretched her neck and departed.

"Your Honor, we have only one more witness to call."

"Proceed," Cappas replied.

"The State calls Emmanuel to testify."

CHAPTER EIGHTEEN

The Judge banged his gavel several times to restore order in the Court. He sent the jury out of the court room.

"In this jurisdiction, unlike some other jurisdictions in this nation, a defendant cannot be compelled to testify," asserted the judge. "If the defendant does agree to testify, he is required to honestly answer any and all questions asked of him. Does the defendant understand this?"

"Yes," responded Emmanuel.

"Will you testify before the Court on this matter?" Judge Cappas asked.

Emmanuel said, "I will testify before God on all matters."

Cappas paused and then replied, "The defendant will testify. Am I to also understand that the prosecution will have no further witnesses to call?"

"Yes, Your Honor, that is correct," Amos responded.

"And will the defense present witnesses?"

Nathan answered, "No."

"I see. Then we will recess until tomorrow morning at which time the defendant will be called to the stand. Following that, we will hear closing statements, and then turn it over to the jury," said Judge Cappas. "Also, given the lack of order in the Court at multiple times during the day, I am clearing the gallery for tomorrow's session. Only reporters approved by me will be allowed to observe the proceedings." He left the bench and the room emptied. Emmanuel was returned to his jail cell.

Nathan, Jamie, and Jonny took the train and went to Felipe's home for the night. On the train ride, they reflected about what would happen tomorrow.

Jonny asked, "Is this God's plan for Emmanuel?"

There was no answer.

The next morning, the three of them took the train back downtown. Even though Jamie and Jonny wouldn't be allowed in the court room, they wanted to be near Emmanuel. Jonny brought Blue to keep him company as they waited outside the Courthouse. When they arrived, an enormous crowd had gathered. People joined hands and bowed their heads in prayer. Nathan went up the long steps to enter the building as Jamie, Jonny, and Blue remained outside.

The lawyers took their places and the jury went to their chairs. Emmanuel entered the room and joined Nathan at the desk. Judge Cappas took his seat at the bench. "The defendant will take the stand. Bailiff, swear in the witness."

Emmanuel walked to the witness stand. The bailiff faced Emmanuel and said, "Do you swear to tell the truth, the whole truth, and nothing but the truth?"

"I know truth and nothing else," Emmanuel stated.

The bailiff looked quizzically at the judge. Cappas frowned and then told the court reporter to note that the defendant was sworn.

Amos methodically approached the witness stand. He put his hand to his chin as if in thought, then asked, "Why are you here?"

"To answer questions."

The prosecutor shook his head in exasperation and said, "No, I don't mean, why are you here in this Court," he said as he amplified his words while spreading his arms out wide, "I mean, why are you here on this planet?"

Emmanuel leaned forward in his chair and repeated his answer, "To answer questions."

Amos started to make an objection to the Judge but then stopped. He looked at Emmanuel and asked another question.

"Who are you?"

"I am the person you are persecuting."

"No, I don't mean that," he again shook his head in frustration. "I mean who are you?"

Emmanuel declared, "I am my Father's Son."

"And is God your Father?"

"God is the Father of all."

"But, are you the Son of God?"

"You've said so. Isn't that why you have brought me to trial?"

Agitated, Amos paced around the well of the Court. "You are under arrest for committing treason and for inciting violence against the State. Some people think you are, in fact, the Son of God, and they are resisting and rejecting their lawful duties as citizens of the State," spoke the prosecutor. "Now, if you want to say this is all a big misunderstanding and that you pledge your loyalty to the State and command your people to likewise display fidelity to this government, take that oath publicly now and we can end this. You can end all of this pain and suffering just by saying those words."

"Do I reject God and accept the ruler of this world as my king?" asked Emmanuel.

"Yes," the prosecutor implored. "Say it, and you will walk this earth under the protection of the State and your followers will kneel at your feet as you lead them in accordance with the directives of the Governor. Say it, say that the Governor of this State is your ruler and your allegiance is to him."

The court room hushed in silence as the jurors waited for Emmanuel's reply.

"No," Emmanuel answered. "I do not accept the ruler of this State as my king. There are no riches or privileges of the State that I seek."

"You reject the ruling power of the Governor and the State's authority over you?" exclaimed Amos.

"I reject the State's claim of authority over me."

"Then do you consider yourself to be above the laws of this good and benevolent State?"

"You say your laws are in the interest of the good. Yet you use your laws to seek my death even though my acts have been only to help and heal in God's name."

"So you claim allegiance to God and to God alone?"

"I am God."

There were audible gasps in the sparsely populated court room. Amos stammered with his follow-up question.

"So you admit it, you claim to be God?"

"I speak openly of my mission. I have done nothing in secret. If you don't believe my words, then believe my works, for they are God's works."

"Ah, yes. The works you have done. Let's talk about a couple of those works." Amos went back to the desk and picked up another file. "Let me see, you claim to be doing God's works. Was it God's work for you to engage in a pretense to steal from the lottery? Was it God's work when you gave a police officer a fake lottery ticket unfairly costing the government millions of dollars?"

Nathan stood up to make an objection. "Your Honor, Mr. Amos is fabricating a lie with his question. It would only cost the State millions of dollars if there never was a winning ticket. Of course, there was a real winning ticket. There had to be, that's why people buy lottery tickets from the government. Someone had to win. Right, Mr. Amos?"

Amos looked at Cappas in confusion. Cappas raised an eyebrow. The prosecutor commented, "Well, I just find it strange that this presumed do-gooder got entangled in a scamming of the lottery."

"Objection, Your Honor, at the characterization by the

prosecutor," Nathan intoned.

"Withdrawn," said Amos. "But I want the defendant to convince the jury that having millions of dollars to exploit for his own means wasn't a great temptation."

Emmanuel said, "What would it profit me, what would it profit any man, to gain the riches of the world but lose his eternal soul?"

Amos struggled to respond and went back to his desk to pick up another file.

"I don't have all the details of how the lottery tickets were fraudulently generated at this time so I will move on to another matter." Amos scanned through another file on his desk. In a grave tone, he asked, "You know a woman named Magdalena."

"Yes," said Emmanuel.

"Do you recall going to a clinic and breaking through secured doors to find this woman?"

Nathan raised another objection. "Your Honor, the prosecution is misrepresenting the facts."

Amos loudly barked, "The facts are that this man charged into a State-authorized medical clinic chasing after a woman and then took a baby and told her it was her child. Those are the facts!" He turned to look Emmanuel squarely in the eyes. "Did you tell that woman that the baby was hers?"

Emmanuel replied softly. "The baby was dead, and, in God's name, was resurrected."

"Does saving a life make it yours to trade?"

Emmanuel did not answer.

Amos continued his barrage, "Did you have the consent of the birth mother to physically remove the baby? Did you have any legal authority to take the baby?"

Emmanuel did not answer.

"I think the jury understands that the answer to those questions is, no." Amos walked back to his desk. "Sir, that is what is called kidnapping." He took a deep breath. "Let me try to make this easy. Right now, we have the woman,

Magdalena, in custody and the baby is with our Dependent Child Welfare Services department. The birth mother has not come forward, and the State has no interest in placing the baby in an orphanage and without maternal care. The State is willing to release the baby to the guardianship of Magdalena assuming, of course, that this woman is not found to be criminally liable. That means the defendant must accept complete responsibility for kidnapping the baby from the clinic. Otherwise, the baby will be taken from Magdalena and placed in DCWS."

Amos walked to the witness stand. He lowered his voice and spoke privately to Emmanuel. "The baby's freedom for yours; that's an exchange the people would approve, don't you agree?"

Nathan stood up to object, Emmanuel lifted his arm with his palm outstretched telling Nathan to stop. Nathan sat down. Emmanuel nodded to Amos in agreement.

Amos said loudly, "Let the record show that the defendant has accepted full and complete responsibility for the kidnapping of the baby known as Lazarus."

Amos slapped the desktop with zeal and exclaimed, "Excellent." He strutted back towards the witness stand. "We are almost through. There are just a couple more things I'd like to know. You said you are here to answer questions. How about this question: if God is all-knowing and all-powerful," he asked, "why did he send you here?" He put his hand on his chin. "I mean, doesn't sending you—the Son of God," he said sarcastically, "doesn't that mean he had made a mistake? If God is perfect, then everything he made is perfect so why would you have to come here to fix things?"

"I am not sent to fix, but to forgive."

"Forgive?"

"I've come to forgive the sins of those who choose to believe in God's word."

"And what will become of those believers whose sins are forgiven?"

"They will be welcomed into God's kingdom."

"What of those who do not believe and who do not seek your forgiveness?"

"Their sins will be retained."

"For how long?"

"Until death."

"And to those unbelievers who carry their sins to their death, what happens to them?"

"Nothing."

"Nothing?"

"Nothing," Emmanuel said. "Death is their ending."

"There's no hell for them to spend in eternity?"

"Eternity without God is hell," Emmanuel said.

Amos stared at Emmanuel for a long time. Finally, he asked, "Will you even forgive those who do you harm?"

"If they are repentant and ask for God's forgiveness and mercy, it is mine to grant." Emmanuel spoke directly to Amos, "Do you ask for God's forgiveness?"

Amos stood before Emmanuel and softly said, "I am seeking your death. Why would you forgive me?"

"Ask and it will be done," Emmanuel said.

The prosecutor opened his mouth to speak, but then closed it without uttering a word. He walked away from Emmanuel.

"One last question," Amos said as he sat down in his chair. "You're on trial for your life. If you are found guilty of treason against the State, you will be hanged. You can avoid all that just by saying the right words in this Court, but you won't. So, I need to ask you: do you want to die?"

"My death was proclaimed the moment of my birth. You may take the life I have in this world, but you have no hold of me when I am raised up in God's kingdom." Emmanuel declared. "This is the purpose for which I was born into the world and the message my life brings, that those who believe in me, believe in God, and shall not perish but have life everlasting."

Amos sat impassively in his chair. After a few moments

of silence, the judge asked if he had any other questions. Amos shook his head, no. Judge Cappas turned to Nathan and asked if he had any questions.

"Yes, I do." He stood up, bowed his head, reflected in silence for a few moments, and then walked slowly to the witness stand. "Actually, I only have one question." He moved even closer to Emmanuel. "That night you walked the streets and found me. I was lost and alone. You came and rescued me. You took me in and you cared for me. You called me friend, you showed me love, you gave me faith. You saved me and made me a child of God." A single tear drop slipped down Nathan's cheek."

"Why?"

Emmanuel reached out and wiped the tear drop away with his finger. He placed his arm on Nathan's shoulder and he answered the question:

"You were suffering and in need. You asked for God's help. I delivered it."

CHAPTER NINETEEN

When Emmanuel finished testifying, Nathan followed him to their place at the table. Judge Cappas watched quietly as Emmanuel walked away from him. Prosecutor Amos stood up and asked the Judge if they should begin with closing arguments. He was instructed to proceed.

Amos stood and faced the jurors. He recounted the State's case against Emmanuel. He told of the deaths and destruction occurring because of the rebellion and argued that they were first instigated by Jona and since perpetuated by Emmanuel. He recalled the laws governing the State and the requirements of all citizens to honor those laws by paying taxes, by adhering to institutional regulations, by obeying the directives of the police force at all times, and by pledging obedience to the executive power of the Governor and his administration. He admonished those who would reject these laws for their own sake and said it was for the common good that the State prevailed and the laws were made. Then he went through the testimony to cite the evidence that proved Emmanuel's guilt. He read from the transcript of Emmanuel's conversation with Judith where Emmanuel rejected the authority of the Governor. He followed that with Emmanuel's testimony on the witness stand where he again rejected the Governor and then claimed himself to be God.

"Can there be any doubt," he asked, "that this man has confessed his treason by publicly rejecting the Governor and rebuking the laws of the State? He said flat-out, you can't serve the Governor if you believe in his God. Then he says that he is God. This man is not only a menace, he is delusional."

He went into the charge of conspiracy to commit fraud in the matter of the lottery ticket. Then he addressed the charge of kidnapping Lazarus.

"There is no judgment for the jury to render," he insisted, "the defendant admitted his guilt."

He concluded his statement by asking the jurors, "What world would you prefer: a world of orderliness and security directed by the benevolent hand of the State or one where every person pursues their own god and everyone is responsible for their own survival without any regard for the needs of others? Don't let his demeanor and reputed kindness confuse you. He has betrayed the State. Your guilty verdict will prove the people's contempt for his teaching. This man is a destructive threat to the world. It is your duty as citizens of the State to reject him. Reject him now; reject him always!"

Amos sat down, his face red from his impassioned speech. The jurors kept their gaze on Amos until he sat down. Then, in anticipation of the case for Emmanuel, they turned their attention to Nathan.

Nathan stood up and walked to the well of the Court. He looked around the room—to the jurors, to the judge, to the prosecutor, to the attendants, to the guards, to the reporters, and to Emmanuel. He gave his witness:

"I'm like you. I grew up in this State. I was taught here. Like you, I worked here. And like you, I had dreams; I had ambition. I had success. But I struggled. And I fought. I suffered. I wandered among the lost. In my wandering, I wondered: who will show me the way?

"One night, I was beaten and left under a tree. Out of the darkness, a light appeared and I was raised up to the light.

"This man, Emmanuel, is the light of the world. I followed him out of the darkness and by him I am saved.

"On an evening just past, my friends and I gathered together with Emmanuel. There were questions asked, for we all have questions. Doubts were expressed, for we all have doubts. And he was asked the question I have asked myself in my wandering, the question you ask yourselves: who will show us the way?

"To this singular question of our lives, he pronounced the one rightful answer: Emmanuel is the way and the truth and the life.

"For Emmanuel is sent to speak the word of God, and Emmanuel is the word of God made flesh.

"And he tells us to know God by knowing his Son.

"And he affirms he is the Son of God by doing works that are born of God.

"And Emmanuel teaches us to forego the temptations of the world and to ask God's forgiveness for our sins.

"And from him we learned that God is love, and love is our calling.

"And he reveals that his body will be sacrificed for the world so that those who follow Emmanuel will see eternal life with God.

"And Emmanuel promises us we will not be alone, for he sends the Holy Spirit who will comfort us and be the Voice of Truth.

"And the day comes when Emmanuel is raised up to the Father and we will follow him home.

"Emmanuel the Christ was sent to deliver us from evil and to deliver us to God.

"The Deliverer reigns.

"God is with us!"

CHAPTER TWENTY

The trial of the State v. Emmanuel was concluded. All that remained was the verdict. Judge Cappas presented the jury with instructions on how to reach a verdict based on the law and the evidence submitted during the case. He sent them to begin their deliberations. It was noon.

Emmanuel was taken to an anteroom behind the court room. Nathan was with him. Guards stood watch. As they were being taken there, Nathan saw Chief Herold pull Judge Cappas into a private room where Governor Platt was waiting. The door was slammed shut, but Herold's shouting could be heard through the walls.

In the corner of the anteroom was a small olive tree in a ceramic pot near a window. Emmanuel went and touched the fruit of the tree. He looked out the window. Below in a barren field behind the Courthouse was a tall platform with a thick wood beam standing vertically at the center and a long rope hanging loose in the wind. Nathan came up to Emmanuel as he gazed at the scene.

"There are a lot of things we can still do, no matter what the verdict is."

Emmanuel turned to Nathan. His eyes were moist. "Am I to forsake my journey when the storm starts to brew? No, this is why I've been sent."

They stood quietly in the room.

An hour later, the bailiff rushed into the Judge's office. The bailiff came out and looked at Emmanuel. "The verdict is in."

Court was called into session. The sanctioned press hurried in to the court room. One reporter shouted out to the awaiting crowd that the jury had reached its verdict. The crowd began to murmur in nervous anticipation.

Amos and his team entered. Emmanuel was led into the room followed by Nathan. Then the jurors slowly entered the court room and went to their seats.

None of them looked at Emmanuel.

Judge Cappas entered. The bailiff commanded all to rise. Cappas sat in his chair. He looked down at the people before him. He turned and looked at Emmanuel. Cappas took a deep breath and asked the jury if it had reached a verdict. A person designated to be the foreman stood. "We have," she said meekly. Cappas asked Emmanuel to rise.

"On the charge of treason against the State, how do you find the defendant?"

The woman looked down at the paper she was holding. Her voice shaking, she stated, "We, the jury, find the defendant, Emmanuel, not guilty."

Cappas put his hands over his face. Amos hung his head. Cappas asked for the jury's finding of the second charge.

"On the charge of conspiracy to commit fraud, how do you find the defendant?"

Again, the woman looked down at the paper and read, "We the jury, find the defendant, not guilty."

Nathan put his hand on Emmanuel's shoulder and awaited the final judgment.

With trepidation, Cappas asked the jury for the last verdict. "On the charge of kidnapping, how do you find the defendant?"

The woman lifted her gaze from the paper. Her eyes

were moist with tears. She started to talk but the words wouldn't come. The Judge repeated his question,

"On the charge of kidnapping, how do you find the defendant?"

She turned to the jurors next to her and extended the paper to them to see if anyone else would announce the verdict. No one came forward.

She turned back to face the Judge. She looked at Emmanuel. He nodded to her.

She cleared her voice and said, "We, the jury, find the defendant, Emmanuel, guilty of the charge of kidnapping."

The entire room was silent. Nathan stood in distress. Cappas flipped through papers on his desk and found the instructions he needed. The Judge looked at Emmanuel. "You have been found guilty of the charge of kidnapping. This is punishable by a minimum sentence of ten years of incarceration. Guards, take the prisoner and return him to his cell pending final processing to the State Penitentiary." Cappas banged the gavel to indicate the end to the trial of the State v. Emmanuel.

Emmanuel stood motionless and stared blankly into space. The guards took him by the arms to drag him to his appointed place. But he wouldn't be moved. He tilted his gaze upward.

Is this the day?

Suddenly, a loud bang was heard coming from behind the court room. Then in quick succession, came two more bangs. Someone yelled, "Gunshots!" Before anyone could move, a squad of armed soldiers invaded the Court. In short order, the room was under the control of the military marauders. Chief Herold pranced into the room.

Judge Cappas looked down at Herold and stammered, "What's going on here?"

"It's time for you to come down from there, now!"

Cappas nervously stepped down from the bench and Herold commanded one of his legion to take the Judge away. Herold stepped up to the bench. He pointed to a reporter. "You, put this on the radio." The reporter did as he was ordered and rapidly turned on his audio equipment. He placed a microphone on the bench and gave Herold the signal to begin.

"For some time, this State has been under siege by this man, Emmanuel; by his predecessor, Jona; and by their misguided followers. I have worked tirelessly to end this abuse of our State. Over the past months, I have had serious disagreements with Governor Platt on how to effectively regain control of this situation. In all cases, Governor Platt has failed to provide the leadership and the courage needed to end this rebellion and restore the just powers of the State.

"This trial which was guided by the Governor's judicial appointee, is the latest, and the last, example of his incompetence and weakness. Now, under my command, the military has taken over the Statehouse. Governor Platt is dead. As of this moment, I am the executive power in the State.

"As your new Governor, I am committed to rooting out all that undermines the good and necessary work of this State. I know that the people of the State will faithfully comply with all their duties under the law once they know the agitators of this wrongful revolt against the State have been captured and punished to the fullest degree.

"This trial presented clear and irrefutable evidence that this man, Emmanuel, has rejected the State and its lawful powers and has, instead, imposed a false deity upon an unwitting population. He has duped the least of our society with baseless promises of salvation. This cannot stand and it will not stand!

"As my first order as Governor, I am invoking martial law. Under martial law, the Governor, as Commander in Chief of the State, has unilateral authority to charge and punish captured enemy combatants. Emmanuel is an enemy of the State and is hereby charged with high treason."

Herold violently banged the gavel and pronounced, "I judge Emmanuel to be guilty of treason against the State. I sentence this man to death by hanging. The execution will commence in the coming hour."

Herold marched off as soldiers took Emmanuel into custody. Nathan tried to follow but was thrust aside.

Outside the Courthouse, throngs of people had waited patiently for news of the verdict. Someone from inside the building had yelled through a window, "Not Guilty." The crowd erupted in cheers.

A minute later, the same person yelled out again, "Not guilty" to more cheers.

Before the verdict on the third charge was announced, platoons of soldiers had surrounded the outside of the building just as their counterparts were invading the court room. More soldiers were seen encircling the Statehouse down the street. Then a radio was turned on and the voice of Herold blared throughout the streets announcing his coup. The people listened in confusion and fear as Herold announced Emmanuel's death sentence.

Armed vehicles pushed through the streets as the military dispersed the crowd. Jamie wanted to leave, but Jonny insisted they be with Emmanuel. They went around to the back of the Courthouse. They were stopped at a locked gate that prevented access to the hangmen's platform. Through the fence they could see preparations being made. A group of people joined Jamie and Jonny. When the stage was set, a soldier opened the gate and let the waiting assembly move into a confined area.

A long line of armed soldiers amassed just steps in front of the platform. Jamie and Jonny were at the front of the crowd.

An hour later, a thick, windowless door opened. On the inside face of the door, was a painted image of the skull and crossbones. A horde of soldiers carrying rifles with shaded visors drawn over their helmets marched in cadence into the killing field. They halted and formed two lines to secure the path. Then a man hobbled out of the building with his feet and arms shackled wearing a drab and torn prison uniform. His eyes were badly bruised and his nose appeared broken. His ripped shirt exposed deep abrasions. Blood dripped from his mouth.

It was Emmanuel.

Next, Herold came out of the door. He said something to Emmanuel but there was no response. He held out his hand and a soldier handed him a long, steel blade. Herold placed it under Emmanuel's chin and raked it down from his neck to his waist completely tearing open his shirt. He took a marker from his pocket and wrote in bold letters on Emmanuel's bloodied chest: The Deliverer.

The chains from Emmanuel's arms were unshackled. They took a thick, wooden beam and laid it across Emmanuel's back. He bore the burden on his shoulders and walked the way of the cross.

Laboriously, he limped along, the blood that dripped from his body marking the path to the place where the cross would be erected. He stumbled, but was held up by a man in the crowd. He kept on, but then fell under the weight of the cross beam. He lifted his head and saw Jonny standing above him. He struggled to speak and said, "My God, have you forsaken me?"

Jonny knelt down, put his face close to Emmanuel, and in a broken voice sang the last verse of the song: "The day is come and God I see." Emmanuel nodded and closed his eyes.

A soldier snatched Emmanuel and pulled him up from the ground. Blue barked and bit at the abuser's ankle. The soldier turned his rifle at the dog, but Jonny grabbed the weapon. The soldier shook off Jonny's grip and shouted, "I'll shoot you both!" and pointed the rifle at him. Instantly, Jamie stepped between them to protect Jonny. The soldier looked at Jamie and then lowered his rifle and walked on.

Emmanuel continued walking the path leading to his

execution. The platform was ten feet off the ground and twenty feet across. There was a lever controlling the trapdoor next to the vertical beam. When the trapdoor opened, Emmanuel would plunge with enough force to sever his spine and cause immediate death. Surrounding the platform was a short wire fence. There was a flight of steps that went up to the platform.

The prisoner approached the stairway. He lifted his foot to go up the steps. One of the guards squawked, "Time to die, oh mighty king!" and shoved Emmanuel forward. The guards' shove sent Emmanuel off balance and he fell hard to the ground with the beam crashing on top of him. The crowd gasped as they witnessed Emmanuel's collapse. Many thought the gruesome fall had killed him. The sentries lifted the cross beam off of Emmanuel and looked down at the limp body below.

Emmanuel stiffly lifted his arm and gripped the first step. He raised himself up. He gazed at the people witnessing his brutal torture. They stared back in silence and in shame.

The man who had helped Emmanuel when he had stumbled came forward again. He took the cross upon himself and walked up the stairway. Two soldiers took Emmanuel by the arm and carried him to the platform. The man who shared the burden of the cross was tossed off the platform by the armed guards.

"Cyrus!" cried out a woman. She ran to her husband and helped him away from the area.

The cross beam was placed into the wide notch of the vertical beam. It was secured with four large bolts. The noose had already been prepared and was attached to an iron hook connected to the underside of the cross beam. A man wearing a black face mask positioned Emmanuel overtop of the trapdoor. The hangman took the noose and loosely placed it around Emmanuel's neck. He tried to pull a dark hood over Emmanuel's head. Emmanuel shook off the hood saying, "The day is come and God I see."

Herold was seen giving instructions to a bald, squat man at the foot of the steps. The unknown accomplice nodded his understanding and then swiftly began working underneath the platform in accordance with Herold's directive. Herold took the stage along with the masked hangman and Emmanuel. He turned and faced the crowd. "Is this your savior?" he shouted. There was no answer until a solitary voice cried out, "We have no savior but the Governor!" Other voices joined in agreement.

Herold grinned slyly and said to Emmanuel, "See how loyal the people are to you? After everything you've done for them, they reject you at your final hour. And now I have the power of life and death. So, I'll ask you one more time. Shall I be merciful?"

Emmanuel turned to Herold and said, "You have no power over me. No power to claim my life and no power to cause my death. Only God has that power. Do what you will."

Incensed at his defiance, Herold turned to the crowd and cackled, "This indigent fool says I have no power over him!" His laughter echoed throughout the killing field. "We'll see about that!" he shrieked as he shoved the hangman away, grabbed the lever himself, and with both hands yanked open the trapdoor.

Emmanuel's limp body plummeted and swung wildly through the air. Screams and wailings emanated from the stunned crowd.

Then a voice cried out, "Look! He's still alive."

The noose had slipped from around Emmanuel's neck. In Herold's frenzy to kill, he had neglected to tighten it. In back of his head, the rope was fixed beneath the base of his skull, as intended. In the front, however, the rope had slipped off his throat and was wrapped around his chin. His head was badly contorted and his mouth was clamped shut. His chest was bulging and his legs were kicking.

Spontaneously, the crowd began pleading to let him loose. One worshipper shouted, "Emmanuel cannot be killed!" Another declared, "He is God!" Others began to call out in chorus, "God is with us! God is with us!"

Herold heard the voices of the people chanting and claiming Emmanuel to be God. He knew his ploy to eradicate Emmanuel from the hearts and minds of the public was at risk. He raced down the steps and grabbed the bald, squat man by the throat and screamed, "Do it now, you idiot!" The man nodded forcefully and hurriedly grabbed a large liquid container. He carelessly poured the entire contents onto a huge pile of kindling wood he had assembled under the trapdoor, directly under the hanging body of Emmanuel.

Rashly, Herold's accomplice lit a match and threw it onto the firewood that was now completely saturated with gasoline. In a split second, a booming explosion shook the entire field behind the Courthouse. A ball of fire cascaded from the platform filling the sky above with searing heat.

The soldiers guarding the gallows were felled by the force of the detonation as the crowds of people fled the rapidly expanding firestorm. Jonny was knocked on his back by the devastating eruption. He scampered to his feet and saw Emmanuel's swaying body engulfed in flames.

"Emmanuel!" Jonny cried out. Jamie held onto his brother tightly as the boy struggled to go to Emmanuel.

But when Jonny collapsed to the ground from the force of the explosion, he lost his grip on Blue's leash.

Freed, the dog sprinted to Emmanuel. From the corner of his eye, Jonny saw Blue dart toward the platform with his leash dragging along the dirt. He desperately lunged for the blue bandana wrapped around the dog's neck.

He couldn't reach it.

"Blue, stop!" the boy screamed in futility. Blue charged the platform and vaulted over the short fence in quest of Emmanuel—his savior. The dog yelped wildly as his body was consumed by the raging blaze. His yelping gave way to silence as he joined Emmanuel in the hellish inferno.

There they were together in this time: a king and his henchmen, a persecuted people, a mother's son born to witness the truth, and a man—the Savior of the world—crucified on the cross.

CHAPTER TWENTY-ONE

The persecution continued long into the night. Governor Herold commanded his militia to swiftly exterminate any acts of insurrection against the State's authority, his authority. They did so with a vengeance, leaving behind the ruins of their evildoings. Armed forces brutally cleared Capital City of any protests, and by evenings' end, had eliminated all resistance. Fires smoldered in the ravaged buildings and a hazy smoke hung in the moonlit sky. Ultimately, an unsettling stillness fell upon the city.

Herold stepped onto the balcony of the Statehouse. He was handed a piece of paper with the speech he would give to the people at the end of his day of fulfillment. He surveyed the burning residue and inhaled the smell of death that permeated the air. He touched the wide bandage covering the facial burns he received from the fire. Even that which had gone wrong, worked to achieve his destiny.

He had ordered that the fire be set after Emmanuel's death, not before. He wanted to ensure that there were no physical remains for his followers to claim. Emmanuel's promise that he would pass from death to life would be proven a fairy tale fiction, determined Herold. It was plain to everyone who witnessed Emmanuel's crucifixion on the cross that there was nothing left of the man.

The newly-crowned Governor of the State gazed upon his kingdom. His publicist directed him to face the camera. The artificial lighting fell upon him and the camera rolled. He read the speech. He ended it by saying, "The reign of Platt is at end. I am the ruler of this world now." The camera was turned off. "The next world is for the fools and the prophets," he muttered as he crumbled the paper and tossed it to the street below.

Thad had gone to Capital City to find his friends. He drove to the Courthouse to get Magdalena. Prosecutor Amos gave Thad the court order directing the release of Magdalena and approving her guardianship of Lazarus. He put them in his truck and slowly navigated the downtown streets. After clearing downtown, he drove along the lake shore looking for Jamie and Jonny. A few miles south, he saw Jamie walking down the street carrying his brother in his arms. Thad helped them into the back of the truck and they drove to Felipe's home.

No one spoke that evening. The morning came and, still, there were no words to express their grief and their loss.

The door opened after a gentle knock and in came Rabbi Nicholas and another man carrying a black leather satchel. Matilda rushed to the Rabbi and he embraced her as she sobbed on his shoulders. The Rabbi introduced his companion.

"This is Giuseppe. He works for the County morgue."

Giuseppe took off his brown derby hat, bowed his head, and said "Con rispetto."

"He doesn't speak much English but he wanted to offer his respects to you all."

Giuseppe then pointed to the satchel.

"Yes," said Nicholas acknowledging his understanding. "After the fire cooled, they brought the remains of the body to the crematorium." He paused as everyone turned their attention to him. "They discarded the ashes." Matilda started to weep again. "When they transported the remains from the fire to the crematorium, they had it…I'm sorry, I mean, they had him, wrapped in a linen cloth. Giuseppe has the cloth in this satchel. Perhaps you would like it as a memorial." Giuseppe extended his arm holding the satchel.

No one came forward.

"Is this how it ends, with a charred cloth from a dead body?" asked Felipe. "Is this the way we all thought it would be?"

"This is not an ending. Emmanuel said this would be his beginning," Nathan responded.

"Yes, that is what he told us," interjected Toma. "But he's not here, and we are. Where does that leave us?"

Nathan said, "It leaves us with everything he taught us and everything he did for us. He told us it would be hard; he told us we would be hated. But he told us what to do and how to be. He told us he would send a Helper. He said we will not be alone. This is our time to become the word of Emmanuel on earth. This is our time to do God's will."

"And how do we do that? What did any of us do yesterday to try and help him? What did he do to help himself? Where were the miracles then?"

Petros interrupted, "I said I would die for him and, in the end, I couldn't even show up to be with him."

"It wasn't just you. We all fall short of what he wanted from us." Toma continued. He shook his head. "I don't know. I'm not even sure that what we saw all this time was real. Did he make the lottery ticket the winner, or was it just luck to get the one-in-a-million ticket? Did he cure the girl in the hospital, or was it just her time to get better on her own? Or, when Blue ran out onto the river, did he walk on the water, or was he just walking on a patch of solid ice…"

"Stop!" Jonny shouted. The disciples fell silent at the command given by their youngest member. He continued:

"Emmanuel saved us. He taught us about loving one another and told us how to find God. He suffered for us and he died for us. He is the Christ. With all that he gave us, can't we be Christians for even a day? Are we going to forget Emmanuel and all that he said and everything he did, now that he's gone? And then go back to the lost and broken lives we had before he came to us?"

Jonny looked around the room at his friends. Angered by their weakness, he implored:

"He gave us everything. What more was he to reveal to us? Tell me, what more was he to reveal?" He waited for an answer that didn't come and then ran out of the house.

They stood in quiet solitude, shamed by their doubts.

After a few minutes, Matilda somberly gathered her things and put them in her bag. She and Rabbi Nicholas would take Giuseppe to his apartment and then head back to Olde Town.

Andy was in the backyard at the pier. He called to his father and asked if they could go out on the boat. Felipe thought that was a good idea. Nathan and Jamie joined them. They grabbed their fishing poles and pushed off into the lake.

Toma wanted to visit a college friend who lived north of Capital City for a few days. Thad said he would take him there. They got in the truck and drove away.

Magdalena had an aunt nearby who wanted to see Lazarus. She walked outdoors and stood on the corner to wait for the bus.

Jonny walked down the road. He sat alone on a patch of grass. He hung his head in sorrow.

Emmanuel, show me the way, he prayed.

He saw his brother and the others on the boat drifting along with their poles in the water. He saw Matilda leave with Rabbi Nicholas. He saw Thad take Toma away in his truck. They had been so close and now, without Emmanuel, they were each traveling separate paths.

He watched as the bus came and he saw Magdalena

board it with Lazarus. She walked to the back to find a seat. He could see her through the large rear window. She saw him, too, and waved goodbye.

The bus started to drive away. Jonny saw Magdalena abruptly redirect her sight. She pressed her face against the glass. Then, Magdalena put her hand over her mouth as she recognized the vision before her. Her face glowed with delight and she held up Lazarus to the window so he could see, too. She put her hand on her heart and nodded in comprehension as the bus continued onward. She waved hello.

Jonny looked away from the departing bus and out upon the lake. The sun sparkled brightly against the calm water and he felt a current of wind rush through him.

Still he prayed:

Emmanuel, show me the way.

"I am the way."

He could hear the words of his faith as if for the first time. Once more, he prayed:

Emmanuel, show me the way.

"I am the way."

Jonny lifted his head. He gazed into a radiant light pervading the sky. He blinked and wiped the brightness from his eyes. He looked into the light and saw a familiar figure. White rays of light poured through the figure, but he recognized the face and he knew the voice.

"Teacher?"

"I am the way and I am the truth and I am life."

Anxiously, he tried to stand and grab hold of the vision, but his legs were trembling and weak. He stared into the brilliance saying, "Emmanuel, is it you? Have you come back?"

"This is what I promised the others and this is what I promised you the day you followed me up the hill. I am born to eternal life."

"But how? You were, I mean, what they did to you, how is it possible?"

"With God, all things are possible."

"Is God with you?"

"God is with us."

"Emmanuel," the young man said with tears streaming down his face. "I thought I lost you."

"I am with you."

He wiped the tears from his eyes as he struggled to get up. "Can I go and tell the others?"

"Yes, go tell the others that I have passed from death unto life. You will bear witness to my promise fulfilled. Jon, now is your time to reveal the truth of my death and new life; reveal it to the world."

He nodded in affirmation. "Will you come and see the others with me? They're on the lake fishing."

"Yes, I will see them and they will see me and they will become fishers of men. They will go to all people in all nations and teach the words I have spoken. And in my Father's name, and in my name, and with the power of the Holy Spirit who follows, those who listen and believe will be born to life everlasting."

Jon headed to the pier.

"I have something for you."

Jon turned around and saw Emmanuel's arm swing majestically towards him. An object floated through the sky and Jon caught it in midair. He looked at the object in his hand.

The blue bandana.

"Blue!" Jon looked at Emmanuel in amazement. "Is he with you?"

"God is love and love endures in God's kingdom."

Jon beamed with elation and ran to tell the others. He stopped once more, turned back, and beheld Emmanuel in the light. He had only one more question.

"Emmanuel," the chronicler asked, "is this the day?"

Emmanuel lifted his face to God the Father with arms outstretched.

Is this the day?

In response, Christ stood beyond the world and acclaimed the triumphant fulfillment of his divine mission:

"This is the day!"

The young man ran shouting and waving to the other disciples on the boat. They heard his call and turned to see the light that was Emmanuel. They saw the truth standing before them and believed. They hailed in exaltation. All of them were witnesses to the resurrection of Emmanuel the Christ, the Son of God.

Jon rejoiced without ceasing and pronounced for all to hear:

"Emmanuel is risen! This is the day!

For the rest of his days, he called to the world in voice and pen testifying that all who believe in Christ will have eternal life with God in Heaven:

"And I am a witness!"

"Let the message of Christ dwell among you richly as you teach and admonish one another with all wisdom through psalms, hymns, and songs from the Spirit, singing to God with gratitude in your hearts."

- Colossians 3:16

ELVO F. BUCCI

ABOUT THE BOOK

An idea came to me for a book. I had never written a book and did not have, or want, a career in literature. I had just finished reading the novel, "Theophilus North" by Thornton Wilder. I enjoyed it because I was captivated by the mystical and enchanting lead character. I told myself that I would like to write a book like that someday.

Over time, I would periodically think about the book but would never get into any significant reflection or plot development. I did, however, write a novel called, "A Perfect War" which is about economic espionage. It sold all of 200 copies, maybe.

Years later, my wife, Marilyn, and I were at Mass at the Catholic Church where we belong when the priest started to read the Gospel. Although I was a regular participant in weekly Mass, I had a tendency to tune out the liturgy. I was tuning it out at the time when I heard the priest recite the passage, "I decided to write an orderly account for you, most excellent Theophilus, so that you may know the certainty of the things you have been taught."

Theophilus—I had not recalled hearing that name in the Bible before. As soon as we got home, I looked up the passage in the Bible. It is from the opening chapter of the Gospel of Luke and introduces the reader to the story of Jesus Christ.

Is the book meant to be about Christ?

I started to think more frequently about the book. Mostly, I started to think more about Jesus Christ. In thinking about Jesus, I concluded that I didn't know as much about him as I had imagined. I had serious doubts writing about someone I didn't know well. I definitely didn't want to write a book about Christ that would disappoint me or disappoint him.

Later on, I helped lead a weekend Men's Retreat in the parish. During our formation process, my friends and I performed a discernment exercise. We sat quietly in the chapel and were asked to reflect upon what we wanted to achieve. The words came quickly to me as I wrote, "I want to reveal myself as a Christian."

With my conviction firmly established, I finally began to write. Through my writing, I came to know Jesus more. I offer this book, the "Songs of the Deliverer" to those who, like me, want to know Jesus more.

The story is my own—you only need the Bible to learn the truth of Jesus Christ—but each chapter in the "Songs of the Deliverer" includes stories and verses with direct parallels to the Gospels: baptism and beliefs, ministry and miracles, the crucifixion and the resurrection. If you are a Christian, you will recognize the scenes, understand the teachings, and know Emmanuel, the man called the Deliverer. Reading the book is time to engage Christ in modern day and to experience the spirituality of the Son of God in a new way.

For those not acquainted with the Biblical stories, the book is a chance to know Christ for the first time. You will soon read that Emmanuel means 'God is with us' and learn why it is true.

To read more about the book the "Songs of the Deliverer" visit the website:

www.songsofthedeliverer.com

ABOUT THE SONGS

Like most people, I enjoy listening to music. I am not a musician, but I have family and friends who have been in the music business. My cousin, Domenic, is a professional musician dating back to his teens. I have followed his performances and productions over the years. My brother, Mark, picked up the guitar when he was in his thirties. He eventually put together a band with his neighborhood pals. I saw a couple of their shows and I have a copy of the album they produced of the songs Mark wrote. Later, Mark played at Sunday services for the congregation of the Evangelical Church where he was a member.

I have a tendency to sing along to songs when I'm driving my car. The problem with that is you can find yourself singing lyrics you don't like. It seemed that, as the years progressed and the music scene changed, there were more and more songs with lyrics that made me uncomfortable.

It finally came to a head one day when I was driving the car with my young children in the back. I started mindlessly singing along to the song on the radio. Then the singer got to the part with the verse, "If you're sexy and you know it clap your hands," and I take both hands off the steering wheel and clap my hands! (Needless to say, my kids were mortified.) I decided something had to change with my musical interests.

About this time, Mark had moved to Indianapolis to join the Indiana School for the Deaf. He trained to be a sign language interpreter and lived on the campus as a teacher and mentor to the students. He loved helping the deaf youngsters and believed he had found his calling in life. (This is the inspiration for Chapter 13 in the "Songs of the Deliverer.")

Then, Mark got sick. He was admitted to the hospital and spent a long time there. Despite countless tests and numerous medical interventions, the hospital could not diagnose a problem and so he was released. A couple days afterwards, he was still feeling poorly and went back to see the doctor. Again, they could not make a diagnosis and sent him away. Later that afternoon, he collapsed in his apartment and died. When they did the autopsy, they found that his stomach was riddled with cancer.

The next day, my sister, Carla, her husband, Paul, and I went to Indianapolis to gather Mark's things. Mark had a car on lease. I drove the car to return it to the dealer with Carla and Paul following me. After driving for a while in silence, I turned on the radio. I knew Mark loved music and he wouldn't mind me listening to some tunes even while mourning his death.

I selected a channel on his presets and a song started to play. It took a few seconds for me to recognize the genre.

It was a Christian song.

But I changed the channel. The next channel I selected on Mark's presets started to play.

It was a Christian song.

I get it.

Ever since then, I've been listening to Christian music. I have hundreds of channels on my car's satellite radio but I only listen to the channel with Christian music.

Now, I sing along in the car loud and proud (and my kids don't mind.)

To read, and hear, more about the songs in the "Songs of the Deliverer" visit the website:

www.songsofthedeliverer.com

ABOUT THE AUTHOR

I am a son.
I am a brother.
I am a friend.
I am a student.
I am an athlete.
I am a worker.
I am a husband.
I am a father.

I am a man called to testify to the truth and the truth is this:

I am a Christian.

I am a believer. I believe in God and in His Son, Jesus Christ, and in the Holy Spirit. I believe that Christ lived and by living he loved and for his love, he was crucified and died. I believe Christ was resurrected from death to deliver those he loved to everlasting life in Heaven.

I am the author of this book. I take these words as my own: Jesus Christ is the way, the truth, and the life.

And I am a witness.

ELVO

Made in the USA
San Bernardino, CA
28 July 2014